# KEEPER OF MY HEART

## DARCY FLYNN

*If you don't break the rules, you miss all the fun!*

*Darcy Flynn*

## SOUL MATE PUBLISHING
New York

KEEPER OF MY HEART
Copyright©2012
DARCY FLYNN

Cover Design by Rae Monet, Inc.

This book is a work of fiction. The names, characters, places, and incidents are the products of the author's imagination or are used fictitiously. Any resemblance to actual events, business establishments, locales, or persons, living or dead, is entirely coincidental.

All rights reserved. No part of this publication may be reproduced, stored in a retrieval system, or transmitted in any form or by any means (electronic, mechanical, photocopying, recording, or otherwise) without the priority written permission of both the copyright owner and the publisher. The only exception is brief quotations in printed reviews.

The scanning, uploading, and distribution of this book via the Internet or via any other means without the permission of the publisher is illegal and punishable by law. Please purchase only authorized electronic editions, and do not participate in or encourage electronic piracy of copyrighted materials. Your support of the author's rights is appreciated.

Published in the United States of America by
Soul Mate Publishing
P.O. Box 24
Macedon, New York, 14502

ISBN: 978-1-61935-148-6
eBook ISBN: 978-1-61935-081-6

www.SoulMatePublishing.com
The publisher does not have any control over and does not assume any responsibility for author or third-party Web sites or their content.

*To the keepers of the light*

*and to the lives they've saved.*

*For my two loves, my husband and my son,*

*who, in their own unique way,*

*stand sentential over my heart.*

# Acknowledgements

Many thanks to the friendly communities of Oxford and St. Michaels, Maryland. Thanks to the off-duty tour guide for the private tour of the Chesapeake Bay Maritime Museum. To Jeff and Cindy McWaters. Those three lovely days in your historic cottage home were sheer delight.

And thanks to my editor, Debby Gilbert, for saying yes.

Special thanks to Cindy Brannam and Sharon Ward-Hermes for your critique and on-target insights. Thanks for being in the trenches with me and for faithfully reading every single word.

Blessings to my wonderful husband, Tom, who was so patient with my late meals and my late nights. And to my terrific son, it is from your darling nine-year-old self that I created my Jamey. I am forever thankful for your sweet childhood, and I am proud of the man you've grown to be.

# Chapter 1

"You sold your paintings for how much?"

Katie pulled the ottoman toward the elderly man who occupied the threadbare chair in the retirement home.

"You're practically giving them away," he said as he placed his elbows on the armrests.

"I haven't exactly sold them yet, Pop. I had to leave Falcon Designs rather quickly or I would have missed the last ferry," she said, plopping down on the footstool.

"But giving up your rights to your art? Was that wise, darlin'?"

"I don't know if it was wise but it was certainly necessary if I'm going to afford the light station. Why, with this plus my savings and the promised loan from the bank, I'll be able to place a more than decent bid. Then I can get you out of here and back where you belong."

"You need to quit worrying about me and finish your degree."

"You know I'm working on that." She sighed as she looked lovingly at the aging man before her. Angus MacAfee was a former Paige Point, Maryland, lighthouse keeper, so to her he was a national treasure. "But I promised Davy I'd take care of you if anything happened to him." Sorrow and regret tugged at her heart.

"Darlin', you were sixteen when he was killed. He wasn't to know that and surely you must know that as your older brother, he would never have placed such a burden on you." A gnarled hand twisted with arthritis patted her forearm.

"First of all, you're not a burden. And it's not just for Davy. It's what I want, too. I shouldn't have even mentioned him." Katie threw up her hands in frustration. Silence filled the small sitting room while they both stared down at the worn, faded carpet.

"So are you hungry? Do you want something to eat?" he asked.

"No, thanks."

"Are you sure? It's clam chowder day, and I have plenty of leftovers. You know Bessie makes the best in town."

"Oh, please not clam chowder," she groaned. "Bessie keeps bringing it to me." Not wanting to seem ungracious, she forced a grin. "She says if I don't stop and eat, I'll blow away in the first nor'easter."

"She's right, you're practically skin and bones. Working two jobs for the past two years—"

Katie raised a slender finger. "Yes, but I already quit my job at Phil's Diner, so I'm only working one now."

"Don't interrupt," Pop said. "Plus going to art classes most of the week, then if that isn't enough, I hear you spend time into the wee hours fixing up that cottage. How you got permission to do that is beyond me."

"Permission? It was sitting there derelict, practically falling to pieces. The town is thrilled I'm fixing it up. Besides, Mr. Davis said I could."

"Henry Davis?"

"Yeah, he says I'll have no trouble acquiring the light station since nobody else seems to want it."

"He actually said that to you?" Astonishment rang in Pop's aged voice.

"More or less."

"Well, if that doesn't beat all I ever heard."

"Relax, Pop. The council meeting is tomorrow night. What could happen between now and then?" Katie tried to sound positive.

"Most people around here think you're mad," he said.

"I know, isn't it great?"

They both laughed.

Sobering, Pop continued. "Katie ... I've given up living at the station again. Maybe you should, too."

"It was your home, and the playground of my childhood. It's going to be ours," she stated emphatically, then leaned forward to kiss his leathery cheek. "I'll see you tomorrow, okay? I'll pick you up before the meeting."

Max Sawyer sped along the county road, deep in thought. It had been three years since he'd been to Paige Point. His stay had been short, about two hours. He'd come to see Katie before his second deployment to Afghanistan. With the risk of death, he'd felt honor bound to reveal his true identity and his connection to her brother, Davy. After two years of letter writing from the warfront, he knew it had been time to tell her the truth. That he was the one driving the car that took her brother's life.

Taking the next turn way too fast, Max's muscles stiffened as he focused on the road before him. In minutes, he pulled up in front of Margaret McCullough's massive Victorian home and let the engine idle.

He recalled how Margaret, Davy, and Katie's aunt had met him at the door of her large estate. Margaret bristled when she saw him. He could still hear her stinging, hurtful words.

"I see you're a Lieutenant, now. Had Davy lived, he might be a Lieutenant today." She'd slammed the door in his face.

Of course now he realized Margaret's scornful reception shouldn't have surprised him. Within hours after the funeral, he'd told Margaret about Davy's last moments, thinking she would want to know. Even though the police had determined it was an accident, clearing him from any wrong doing, in some twisted way, Margaret had still blamed him for Davy's death.

Although he'd continued writing to Katie, he'd never received another letter from her. Until then, he hadn't realized how much she'd meant to him. But last week, after three years of silence, he received a letter from her. She still addressed him as 'Her Sailor.' Why?

Margaret had to have told her who he was. But he couldn't deny the small hope that surged within him. Intrigued, he decided on a change of plans. He would still buy the light station, fulfilling his own self-imposed obligation to her and to Davy, but now he would stay in Paige Point and personally oversee the renovation of the property. He would still keep his identity a secret. That part would be easy, since Katie had never known his name or what he'd looked. After all these years, he wasn't sure he'd recognize her, either, but in a town this small, she shouldn't be too hard to find. But first, he had to see the Mayor and place his bid.

Katie peddled down the hill from the retirement home, her mind on things other than the traffic. Her cell phone chimed with a message. Unable to resist, she pulled it out of her pocket to glance at the caller ID. She heard a screeching of tires. Her breath shot out of her as a car struck the end of her bike, throwing her body onto a car fender, sending a shock of pain through her shoulder and right hip. She rolled off the car into a nearby ditch, twigs and stones scraping her exposed skin. Momentarily stunned, she lay dazed for a second before she heard car doors slamming and running feet approaching from more than one direction.

"Are you all right?"

She heard a woman's and a man's voice ask simultaneously.

"Yes ... I think so." She tried to push her bruised body up off the ground.

"Are you sure you're okay?" A stranger hunkered down beside her, his eyes dark with concern.

"I think so."

"Nothing sprained or broken?" The terse question came as he ran his hands over her shaken body in what felt like an expert fashion.

She gazed up at the most gorgeous golden-brown eyes she'd ever seen. No, not brown. More like mahogany with a splash of honey in their depths. Heart thudding and breathless, she opened her mouth to thank the stranger.

"What the heck were you thinking? You turned right in front of two cars."

Stunned, Katie blinked. The splash of honey had turned to fiery chips, glaring down at her.

"He's right, miss," stated the woman who'd spoken earlier. "You turned your bike right out in front of us."

"I'm really sorry. I was just ..."

"Text messaging," the stranger ground out.

Katie felt her cheeks flush at the reprimand. "I was not text messaging."

Clearly exasperated, he hauled her the rest of the way up onto her feet while the woman hurried back to her car.

"Hey, that hurt." Katie scowled up at his hard features. "Do you have to be so rough? What if I'd sprained something?"

"You're all right."

"Oh, yeah, tell that to my shoulder you just pulled out of its socket." She grabbed hold of her upper arm.

Ignoring her, he strode over to her twisted bike. He pulled it off the ground much like he'd yanked her up. Without a word, he set the front fender between his strong legs, and with a few twists and turns straightened out the front tire.

"Here, that will at least get you home." He set the bike in front of him, indicating with his head she should take it.

She snatched the bike from his secure hold and glared at him, her unexpected lack of gratitude surprising even her. *Could it be that he'd hit the nail on the head when he'd said you'd been text messaging?* She shoved her conscience aside, then forced her expression to soften.

He gave her a long, considering look. Then something seemed to strike him as humorous because his hard features relaxed, and a slow smile formed on his lips that just moments ago were thinned in anger. Suddenly breathless, her heart caught in her throat. His smile reached into his deep-set eyes, bringing a subtle twinkle to their depths.

Katie lifted her chin, making a valiant attempt to hold onto her dignity and her temper. He *would* have to look like some Greek god. She scrambled onto her bike and peddled off as quickly as her shaking legs would carry her, refusing to glance behind her at the man she knew was watching her. She scolded herself as she panted to make it up the hill, telling herself with each push on the pedals that her breathless state was caused by the steep uphill climb, not by a pair of amber eyes that had the power to look right through her.

Katie peddled her bike directly to Mike's Bikes and after hearing the repair costs, left it for the time being. Her sandals clicked against the wooden planks as she walked to Rods n' Reels, the hardware/tackle shop where she worked on Saturdays. Several lean cats prowled nearby. They knew what time the daily catch would be arriving. Soon these docks would be filled with fishermen and the local chefs and grocers, ready to buy an assortment of fresh gifts from the sea.

There were several customers in the store when she went in. Lily was at the checkout counter and waved as Katie passed by. At five foot four, her red hair cut in a short cluster of curls, she looked much younger than her forty-two years.

Lily's smile faded on her face when she spotted her. "Hey, what happened to you?"

"Tell you later." Katie hurried to her attic apartment, biting back a groan at each step. She'd have to take some pain reliever.

Once inside, she stripped off her clothes and turned on the shower. While she waited for the water to warm up, she looked at herself in the bathroom mirror, then grimaced. Streaks of dried blood feathered across her right forearm and she could already see red splotchy whelps forming on her right thigh. She gently pushed her fingers against the bruise and winced.

Slowly, her coltish reflection began to fade from sight as the mirror fogged up from the hot steam. She adjusted the temperature, then stepped under the soothing warmth. She was exhausted. And not only from the accident. The past two years had taken its toll on her physically and emotionally. She let out a long sigh. *Please, God, let this all work out.*

## Chapter 2

Dressed in white shorts and a pink T-shirt, Katie rummaged through her closet for her Keds. Still in good condition, the old white canvas sneakers had belonged to her mother, and Katie loved wearing them. She tied the laces and thought about what supplies she needed to grab from downstairs.

"One gallon of paint, three-inch brush ... is that everything, Katie?" Lily asked.

"Yep."

"Oh, I almost forgot. Your hinges came in this morning." She picked up the house phone to call storage, then returned her attention to Katie.

"How's it going at the cottage? Are you almost finished?"

Katie laughed. "Never finished. You know how it is."

The bell hanging on the front door rang as a customer entered.

"Be with you in a moment," Lily called out. Lily's husband, Tom, his wide, easy grin flashing like a light from his bearded face, approached the counter with the box of hinges. His tanned and rugged features gave him the appearance of the sailors of old.

"I'll put these in your Jeep, Katie."

"Thanks, Captain," she teased as they walked out the back of the store. "Do you still think I made a mistake investing so much time and money in the station?"

Tom shrugged. "I'm just worried you could lose everything you've invested if you're outbid."

"Now you're beginning to sound like Pop."

"I would have done it differently, that's all. I'm not much of a risk taker," Tom said, slamming down the back hatch. "I would have saved my money *and* my energy until I actually owned the place."

"Where's the fun in that?" Katie laughed, then hugged Tom goodbye.

After grabbing a sandwich and a drink at Paige's Market, Katie pulled into the curved oyster shell driveway marking the entrance to the light station. The quintessential compound of gray clapboard cottages with its white picket fencing welcomed Katie as her gaze fell on the tower standing sentinel in the distance. Using old black-and-white photographs as her guide, she had worked painstakingly over the past two years to restore the buildings and the grounds as her limited funds would allow. It had taken her months to refurbish the fence, even bartering with some of her paintings for the lumber and installation.

She stepped out onto the late October lawn. Although it was autumn, most of the perennial garden was still in bloom, white Coneflowers, Black-Eyed Susans, the intense blue-violet of salvia, and dark pink Rugosa roses forming a background hedge connecting the two houses together. The clematis, although no longer in bloom, still displayed its green foliage in a trailing mass along the fence, its sticky tendrils climbing up the side of the cottage as well.

As always, the tower beckoned. Sheer joy spread through her veins as she turned and looked up at the light. She couldn't help it. It had been days since she'd been up there. In seconds, she was running up the spiral staircase, taking two at a time, stopping only briefly to transfer a quick kiss from her lips to her fingers to the heart on the wall. Out of breath and laughing, she stepped out onto the platform. The Chesapeake Bay spanned before her. Flanking the water's edge were masses of colorful hardwood trees rich in oranges and yellows that held their own against the daily vibrant sunsets. The sun's reflection off the water seemed to wink at her as she left the tower exhilarated and filled with hope.

She set to work removing the existing rusted and broken hinges in the cottage. An hour later, she collapsed onto the stuffed chair and glanced at her wristwatch. Almost four-thirty. No wonder she was starving.

Taking a bite out of her sandwich, she looked with satisfaction around the cozy living space. Antique pine floors, mellowed with age, were covered with hooked rugs. The chintz-covered sofa and the striped chair were both flea market finds as well as the small coffee table nestled between them. How different it was from the keeper's quarters, which housed most of the furniture that had belonged to her parents. The cottage was uniquely hers. She took a last swig on her water bottle to wash down the rest of her sandwich, then got back to work.

She had just started painting the WELCOME POP sign when she heard a familiar voice call her name.

"Hello. Are you in there?"

As promised, her best friend, Jill, had arrived to help. Barking ensued as Katie ran to open the door.

"Buddy." Katie dropped to the floor and threw her arms around the furry neck of her golden retriever. She stood to give Jill a welcoming hug, as Buddy jumped up on both of them.

"He's missed you."

"I hadn't noticed." Katie laughed.

Jill followed Buddy through the cottage, exclaiming over Katie's color choices and flea market finds with enthusiasm. "Pop will love it."

"I was just making a welcome banner for him. Here, take a brush and paint some sea shells in the corners while I finish the lettering."

Buddy settled himself on one of the rugs while she and Jill commenced working. Although Jill, a fashion design major, had grown up in the area, Katie hadn't met her until they'd taken an art class together. Pretty and perky, Jill's short, dark-headed frame was slightly rounded and full of energy.

"I brought you an extra copy of that article on you from last month's *American Artist* magazine," Jill said as she tossed it on the table. "So what happened with your meeting this morning?"

"Gosh Jill, it's not a hundred percent certain, but Falcon Designs has basically commissioned me to paint six water colors based on my lighthouse drawings and"—She held up her hand before Jill could utter a word—"They're going to be displayed in a new line of exclusive hotels."

"Katie, that's great."

"Thanks. This is huge for me, and the sale of my paintings couldn't have come at a more perfect time."

"I know. I'm so keeping my fingers crossed for you. It's like you've always said, 'Hard work applied ...'"

"...No dream denied," they ended in unison.

## Chapter 3

Friday's sunrise, streaming through the attic room curtains, promised a beautiful day. There was so much to get done before tonight's meeting. Katie pulled a ball cap over her head and drove to the compound. Setting the rickety ladder as close to the house as she could, she tentatively mounted the first rung until she got used to the slight swaying beneath her and began to paint.

She worked non-stop for about two hours, periodically adjusting the position of the ladder. Beads of sweat trickled down her back as she climbed down to move the ladder farther to the left. Back up near the top, Katie stretched upward to reach the corner of the window and with a steady hand smoothed the gleaming white along the newly sanded surface.

"Who gave you permission to paint this building?"

Startled, Katie peeked underneath her arm, still stretched above her head. Momentarily stunned, she stared down at the infuriating stranger from the day before. He stood, hands on hips, plainly put out with her. Katie lowered her arm and clung to the rungs of the ladder.

"The city council gave me permission," she answered hesitantly.

"Come down before you break your neck."

Aghast, Katie felt her mouth drop open and color rush to her face. "Who do you think you are?"

"Now." He pointed one long finger to the ground below her. "We need to talk."

Her mouth clamped shut as she seethed in anger at

his dictatorial manner. She had a thing or two to say to him herself. "Fine," she snapped, wondering what this could be about. She reached around the ladder to grab the handle on the gallon of paint.

"Leave it."

Fuming, Katie made as if to release the handle but instead jerked on it, tipping some of the contents toward him. Like a feline on the docks, he jumped out of harm's way with only seconds to spare, the white paint slightly splattering his right pant leg.

He muttered an oath, then glared up at her.

Katie's eyes widened as she watched him slowly approach the ladder and take a step up. He was on the second rung when she squeaked, "Okay, okay, I'm coming."

She waited until he was off the ladder, but for some reason she couldn't move.

"If I have to start up that ladder again—"

She felt her eyes widen, then narrow. "Are you threatening me?"

"If trying to keep you from breaking your neck is a threat, then yes."

She was never one to back down, but after a brief moment of clashing 'wills' and the fact that she had no where to go but down, she decided the wiser course of action was to do as he said. With a defiant lift of her chin, she slowly descended the ladder.

She no sooner hit the ground before he grabbed her arm and hauled her across the grass to the front of the house. Katie had to take several small steps to keep up with his long stride. When they stopped, she stared up at him with trepidation. She was alone today. With no makeup on and her hair pulled back in a ponytail, she knew she looked like a kid. He raised his hand and lightly tipped off her ball cap.

"I thought it was you." He gave her a gentle push down onto one of the garden chairs and strode over to the nearby spigot. Grabbing the paper towels she always had ready for emergencies, he pulled off a wad and commenced scrubbing his stained pants, eyeing her meaningfully.

Katie gave a quick glance at her Jeep parked nearby and wondered if she should try and make a run for it.

"Don't even think about it," came that irritatingly controlled voice.

*What was this uncanny way he had of reading her thoughts?*

Straightening, he stalked over to the garden table, yanked out the chair opposite hers, and sat down. "Now, what do you mean, you have permission to paint this structure?"

"Just that." She raised her chin, determined not to reveal any information she didn't have to as she surmised he must be here in some official capacity. Although, at this late date, she wasn't about to jeopardize her chances of acquiring the light station because of some technical glitch. She felt she needed to clarify. "Look, I'm acting on the authority of Henry Davis, the chairman of—"

"The town council, I know. I've met Mr. Davis." He eyed her thoughtfully. "So you're aware of the bid on this property?"

"Of course I'm aware, I'm the—"

"Look, no one should be working on this property now that there is a firm bid on the place."

Katie folded her arms across her chest in mock resignation. "Okay, fine by me." She shrugged. *And as soon as you're gone, buster, I'll finish my work.*

The stranger glanced at his watch, then rose to his feet. "Right then. I don't want you back on that ladder or doing anything more on this property. And please see that this stuff is cleared away. I'm late for a meeting with Mr. Davis now or I would do it."

Katie was truly perplexed and decided it was probably better to go along with whatever Mr. High and Mighty requested until she owned the station. Then she could do as she darn well pleased.

"Of course," she answered pleasantly enough, though she was beginning to boil inside. "And who knows," she continued, "maybe the new owner will hire me on and then I can finish the painting."

He looked at her, a mocking light now evident in his brown eyes. "Maybe he will at that."

"Oh, and what if *he* turns out to be a *she*?" Katie couldn't resist asking.

"Trust me, that won't be happening."

Katie fumed inwardly at his arrogant, chauvinistic nerve. After he left, she defiantly mounted the ladder and finished up the window. As she worked, a gleeful satisfaction surged through her at the thought of him discovering *she* was the bidder.

Katie took one last walk through the cottage. She had already brought a few personal items over from the apartment and the welcome banner was taped over the doorframe to the little parlor. The table was set for a celebration tea. Scones were stacked in a glass-covered dish and fresh sandwiches were in the refrigerator.

"Looks like a showroom for *Cottage Living* magazine."

"Jill," Katie squealed in delight. "You came."

"Of course I came and ... I also brought you your notes. You weren't in class today, you bad girl." Jill shook her finger in mock reprimand. Raising her delicately plucked eyebrows at Katie's appearance, Jill said, "I can see you're running late, so why don't I pick up Pop and meet you there."

"Would you?"

"Yes, and I'll take Buddy, too. They'll love having him at the retirement home for a while."

Katie arrived feeling a bit harried but hoped she still managed to look fresh in white jeans, a red-and-white stripped sweater and her docksides. There was a hum of voices in the hall as the townspeople gathered, their chairs scraping and papers rustling.

"What kept you?" Jill demanded as Katie quickly sat between her and Pop.

"I stopped by Davy's tree. And there was a last minute customer. A pipe burst or something. I was locking up for Tom and Lily and hadn't the heart to turn him away. The poor guy's ceiling caved in." She pushed a strand of hair behind her ear and smiled over at Pop while Jill continued.

"Mr. Davis was looking for you earlier. He seemed agitated. Said he needed to talk to you before the meeting started and that it was extremely important."

Katie's heart plummeted. *Had something changed? He'd told her they were all set.*

The pounding of the gavel quieted the crowed room, and Mr. Davis called the meeting to order. "It is community concern like yours that makes our small town such a special place to live and to raise our families," the chairman crowed with obvious pleasure. "Our first order of business ..."

Katie was only half listening as she chewed on her soft bottom lip in nervous anticipation. Two years. Two whole years of working two jobs, not buying anything, except the bare essentials. It had been tough, but worth it. The lighthouse meant everything to her.

The scattering of applause fanning across the room caught Katie's attention.

She looked up as Mr. Davis mopped his brow with a handkerchief. His brief apologetic look sent her pulse skyrocketing. Something was wrong.

Clearing his voice, he continued. "Next on the schedule is the business of the lighthouse property. As most of you know, the Kendrick family bought the light station in the early 1950s, after the U.S. Coast Guard decommissioned it. When Nathan Kendrick passed away ten years ago, the will stipulated that the station would be donated to the town. But due to the unfortunate vandalism to the buildings and the lack of funds, the city was unable to care for the property. As most of you know, the light station sat derelict until one of our very own volunteered to bring order to the buildings and the grounds." He paused, then yanked his outdated narrow tie away from his chubby neck. "The committee most humbly thanks this person for all of her care and management of the station."

A slow chill crept of Katie's back. *Something's very wrong.* She sat clutching her hands tightly in her lap.

Mr. Davis stopped to take a sip from his glass of water. He cleared his throat, glanced in Katie's direction, and then, on a resigned sigh, he continued.

"We, the committee, feel fortunate to have received two bids for Paige Point Light Station." This time he looked out across the hall of faces and locked his gaze with hers.

Katie sat stunned. She felt the blood drain from her face and a dizzying sickness gripped her stomach. She heard Jill's sharp intake of breath.

"So it is with great pleasure I announce that the light station is awarded to M.F.S. Enterprise, one of the nation's premier developers of historic properties."

Sporadic applause broke out across the room.

Tears welled up in Katie's eyes, threatening to spill over any second. She sat perfectly still, struggling to maintain her composure. She could feel the pity-filled glances of those around her, and she found herself giving brief, trembling smiles to them in an attempt to cover up her shock.

"Max Sawyer, the owner of the company, is here tonight and would like to say a few words," Mr. Davis said.

With that, a tall figure at the back of the room stood. Katie turned her head with the rest of the people in the room.

Her heart plummeted as she watched the stranger from the lighthouse walk toward the podium. Suddenly the thought of sitting there another second was more than she could bear.

"Pop," she whispered with urgency.

Aged, but perceptive blue eyes met hers with understanding through his weather-beaten face.

"Come, Katie." He stood and grabbed her arm for support. With a grateful heart, she assisted him to the door closest to their seats. Jill followed them outside, then left with the promise that she'd do an Internet search on Max Sawyer.

The short drive back to the retirement home was a somber one for Katie. Not even Buddy's joyful greeting upon their arrival could lift her mood.

Several minutes after dropping Pop off, Katie pulled up to the cottage, which was bright in welcome, since she'd left the lights on earlier. She hoped she'd have time to get the smaller personal items out before *he* arrived. She owned everything in both dwellings and how she was going to deal with that without acute embarrassment, was beyond her at the moment.

She left Buddy in her vehicle and walked up to the door that she'd thought would be hers. The door she'd caulked and painted. She turned the key she no longer owned in the lock she'd bought and installed, then stepped inside the compact kitchen she'd reverently restored. Swiping at a tear, she quickly grabbed a sack from under the sink and walked into the parlor. She took the photos from the shelves and placed them in the bag. The rest of her belongings would pass as general decorative items for now.

After removing the few items from her closet, Katie picked up a treasured photo of her with Davy when she was fifteen and he was twenty-one. They were standing on the dock with Page Point Light just behind them. Her face suddenly crumbled as she lovingly placed it in the top of the sack. She walked back into the kitchen feeling the weight of the bag and set in on top of the kitchen table. As she took one more walk through, she told herself that it was to make sure there were no more obvious personal items left, but she knew it was to memorize every inch of every corner before everything changed. Lifting her eyes to the banner, she ripped it off the doorframe, then crushed it up in her hands.

"Excuse me." Max Sawyer spoke from behind her.

Startled, Katie swung around. She was so absorbed in her task she hadn't heard him come in. Standing frozen, she felt sheer humiliation spreading through her veins.

Max's tall frame filled the cottage doorway, dwarfing the small kitchen. Even in her distress, she was fully aware of his broad shoulders and had a sudden desperate longing to throw herself against him and plead with him to retract his bid.

Max studied her, his gaze fixing on her face. "Are you all right?" He took a step toward her.

Collecting herself, she turned her back to him.

"Yes, I was just getting the place straightened up for you," she said, unable to look him in the eye and rubbing her hands up and down the sides of her pants in an attempt to calm herself. She would not make a fool of herself in front of the man who'd stolen her lighthouse out from under her. When she felt composed, she turned around again.

"Here are the keys." She held the set toward him, keeping her gaze fixed on the top button of his shirt.

"Oh, so you're the one Henry Davis mentioned this evening."

Startled, Katie's eyes flew to his.

"The one he thanked for keeping the place up." At her nod, he continued. "I take it that's why you were painting the house. I'm Max Sawyer, by the way," he said as he put out his hand.

The last thing she wanted to do was shake this guy's hand. She hesitated only briefly, then placed her hand in his. "I'm Katie. Katie McCullough."

His warm grip tightened, then suddenly stilled at her words. Katie raised her eyes to his face. The penetrating stare he was giving her was unnerving to say the least. She couldn't be certain, but thought she'd glimpsed a momentary look of shock in his eyes. But why? She'd never met him before in her life.

Caught completely off guard, Max hadn't given much thought as to how he'd respond when he found her. He certainly didn't think he'd end up staring at her like some speechless fool. She was no longer the teenager he'd held in the tower. She was lovely. All grown up. All golden and coltish. Feisty and headstrong. Why hadn't he noticed before? He should have known she was his Katie. From the moment yesterday when he'd picked her up off the ground to just now, when he'd walked into the kitchen and saw her in tears, the urge to comfort her had been overwhelming. He released her hand and walked into the little parlor.

"This really looks great. Much better than I expected," he said as he glanced back over his shoulder, wondering what had upset her. If he could keep her talking, maybe he'd find out.

"And just what were you expecting?" She sniffed.

"Oh, I don't know ... paint peeling off the walls, termites even. It's obviously been well maintained, a bit feminine for my tastes, but nice." Damn, he was babbling like a teenager on his first date.

Katie stopped in her tracks. "I'm glad you find it to your liking." Her words tumbled out in a rush. Grabbing the sack, she all but ran to the door.

"Wait. Aren't you going to show me the upstairs? Here, let me carry that."

She looked up at him and clutched her burden tightly to her chest. His gaze held hers as he peeled her hands away from the sack. In the two years he'd written her, he'd never known her eyes were such a dazzling blue. He experienced a moment of regret never having exchanged photos with her. He recalled how he'd insisted on total anonymity, which, lucky for him, she'd found intriguing. What sixteen-year-old girl wouldn't? He knew she'd keep writing him after that.

It was all he could do not to take her in his arms. But he couldn't, not yet. Even though her tears were now gone, her pain was raw. An open wound mingled with anger. Was it toward him? Could she possibly know who he was?

As he held the sack, he nodded toward the staircase. "Why don't you show me around upstairs before you go?" He watched her eyes fill with sheer panic as she glanced between him and the door. Without taking his eyes from her, he inched backward. Finally, she moved toward him with a tentative step. Max got the distinct feeling that if he hadn't stepped away when he did, Katie would have snatched the sack from his arms before bolting for the door. She was obviously hell bent on leaving. As he turned and continued up the steps, he didn't glance back, just listened for her footsteps.

Katie followed him up the stairs, then led him through each room. Even stiff and uncertain, she was beautiful.

"As you can see, there are three bedrooms, those two are connected by a large bathroom. At this end of the hall, is another bedroom."

Love infused her voice as she spoke about Pop's place.

"Oh," he said, feeling awkward and embarrassed for a reason he didn't quite understand. "And each has its own bathroom. I like it."

He followed her out of the bedroom to the landing.

They stopped and looked out of the large paned window at the lighthouse. "It's really beautiful, isn't it? Holding court over all it surveys."

He glanced at Katie expecting a reply, but she was silent. Her face was filled with a sad radiance he found captivating. Afraid she would start to cry, he asked, "Where do those steps lead?"

"To the attic and the captain's walk. Look, it's getting late, and I need to get going."

"Of course. I'm sorry if I kept you too long." But his words fell on deaf ears, as she was halfway down the staircase.

Neither spoke as they went outside. Max placed the sack in the Jeep, while Katie climbed behind the wheel. He stepped around to the driver's side and rested his hands on the door, wracking his brain for something to say to delay her departure.

"Thanks for bringing the keys." When she didn't respond, he added, "I'm sure I'll see you around. Goodnight, Katie."

She gave a quick nod and pulled out of the compound.

Max stuffed his hands deep within his pockets and watched Davy's kid sister disappear down the drive. As he turned to walk back inside, he stopped and looked up at the lighthouse. He stood motionless and thought about the first time he'd met her. It was a dark night with just enough moonlight to mark his path up the spiral steps. His heart still lurched within him at the memory of her broken sobs filtering down from the lofty height of the tower. Clenching his jaw at the raw feeling of guilt still taunting his insides, he slowly mounted the cottage steps, wondering what could have happened to upset her. Back inside, he noticed a large wad of paper on the floor. He picked it up, then smoothed the banner out on the table. He read POP. WELCOME TO OUR NEW HOME.

## Chapter 4

Katie found the cool breeze soothing as she sped to her little island knoll four miles off shore. Although the rustic one-room cabin had no electricity and only an underground pump for water, it held many happy childhood memories of camping with her family. As she neared the shore, she shut off the boat's motor and let the dinghy glide onto the sandy bank. Pulling the boat farther up onto the sand, she secured it with a rope to a tree stump, then unloaded the supplies.

A strong, musty odor filled her senses when she opened the cabin door. On further inspection, she discovered the roof had leaked onto the top bunk, ruining the mattress. After hauling the offending mass outside, she opened the windows to air out the cabin. She would repair the roof tomorrow.

That night, robotic and emotionless, she gathered wood for the campfire with Buddy's help, but mostly he carried a stick around in his mouth while she did all of the work. Finally, the smell of roasting hot dogs filled the night air. Except for the occasional thump of Buddy's tail, Katie ate in silence, then shoved the last bit of bun between her lips, before walking over to the water's edge. She slid to the ground and drew her knees to her chest.

Gazing at the lighthouse, she began to count. "One, two, three, four-and-a-half seconds. Always four-and-a-half seconds—the light's signature. Bet you didn't know that, Buddy." Tears coursed down her cheeks, as uncontrollable sobs broke from her lips. She lowered her head to her knees and grieved the loss of her beloved light station.

"Katie, you can't hide in the stock room all day," Lily said as she stepped through the doorway. "These people have watched you grow up. They mean well, but sometimes they just aren't very sensitive. Besides, I really need you back on the floor. You know how it is on Saturdays."

Katie glanced up from the floor where she was stocking the bottom shelf with air filters. "But everyone is staring at me and whispering. I can't go back out there. I can't stand another 'Why, we're so sorry, Katie. We heard he outbid you, Katie. What are you going to do now, Katie? Honestly, Lily, I'm so depressed. I just want to cry, but it seems like the whole town needs light bulbs today."

Lily stifled a grin and pushed Katie back out onto the sales floor. "You've cried plenty already, honey. But I've seen you bounce back from worse than this. And I know it's not much, but you can have the attic apartment as long as you need it. How is your commission coming, by the way?"

"I haven't heard anything back yet. I'm actually beginning to get a little worried. But I know when the deadline is, so I'm just plugging away toward that end."

"Well, I think you should concentrate on that for the time being." Lily gave her a hug of encouragement.

As soon as Katie walked behind the counter, Bessie and her sister, Mrs. G, came in the store and approached the counter. "Katie, this is my younger sister, Kathy Gibson."

"I know. Hey, Mrs. G." Katie faced Bessie with a smile. "Mrs. G was my ninth grade English teacher, remember?"

"Hello, Katie, it's nice to see you again."

Mrs. G's compliment and Bessie's, "Oh, that's right, I remember now," came at the same time.

"Thanks. Anything I can help you with?" Katie hoped to keep the subject on hardware supplies.

"No, honey, we're fine." Then Bessie's ample bosom leaned into the counter. *Here it comes.* Katie groaned inwardly.

"I heard what happened," she whispered. "I'm so sorry, dear. I know how hard you've worked and how much owning the light station meant to you."

"Thanks, Bessie."

"And don't you worry yourself about Angus." Bessie patted Katie's hand in affection. "I'll take good care of him until you figure out what you'll be doing next."

Katie fluttered a weak smile in return.

During her lunch break, Katie fingered the station keys in her jeans pocket. At some point she'd have to relinquish these as well, but as long as her personal possessions were still on the station, she'd have to keep them a while longer. Besides, no one would know. And when she figured out how to get her things out, she would give him this set of keys as well.

Katie worked the counter and assisted several customers during the rest of the afternoon. Shortly before closing time, the bell on the door chimed. She looked up from where she was leaning on the counter, chin in her hands, and watched as her new enemy entered the building. With the casual grace of a leopard, Max Sawyer strolled down the aisle to the back of the store. The mere sight of him yanked her right off her self-pity merry-go-round.

*What did he want?* She'd outfitted that cottage with everything it could possibly need, unless he wanted to replace all of the chrome fixtures with nickel. She so didn't want to wait on him. Katie frantically looked around for Lily, anyone to rescue her.

"Katie." The deep resonance of his voice plunged her heart into erratic thumping. "I didn't know you worked here?"

Katie glanced up briefly and met his enigmatic expression. "Yes, every Saturday." She looked at the hammer in his hands. "Why do you need this? There's a hammer in the tool chest at the cottage."

"I know, but it's too small."

"Oh. Will this be all then?"

"No, I need two one-hundred-foot garden hoses. There weren't any on the shelves. Do you have any in the back by any chance?"

Frowning hard at him, she picked up the house phone. "Tom or Lily, pick up, please." While she waited, she covertly watched Max Sawyer pull out his cell phone and check for messages. He was casually dressed in faded jeans and a well worn, white cotton, collared shirt. The sleeves were rolled up to the elbows, showing off his tanned forearms and capable-looking hands. She felt suddenly and inexplicably drawn to him.

He glanced over at her, and their eyes locked. The corner of his mouth twitched and he raised a questioning eyebrow at her.

"Katie ... Katie, are you there?"

Flustered, Katie answered. "Uh, yes, Tom. Do we have any more one-hundred-foot hoses? "

She paused, giving Tom a minute to find out. "He's checking."

"By the way, the scones and sandwiches were delicious."

Katie scowled. She'd forgotten all about her scones.

"But somehow I get the feeling that you'd rather I'd choked on them." He flashed her a smile, and she wondered again how he could read her mind so accurately.

"Look, I'm sorry I jumped all over you yesterday," he said.

Katie's breath caught in her throat. *He was apologizing?*

"Call me old-fashioned, but I stand by the fact that little girls shouldn't be dangling from the tops of ladders, rickety or otherwise. Am I forgiven?" His brown eyes held a twinkle in their depths.

The ringing of Max's phone startled her. "Excuse me," he said as he walked a few feet away to take his call.

"Oh, I can tell he's real sorry," she muttered to herself.

"What do you mean she's disappeared?" Katie heard him say into his phone.

Who disappeared? she wondered.

Lily was locking the door so no one else could come in when Tom walked up with the two long hoses. "Last two." He smiled, then leaned toward her. "Hey, Kate," he whispered. "Is that the guy?" Katie groaned and nodded her head, letting out a long sigh.

"Sorry," Max said as he returned to the counter. "Business associate. Oh, great you had them." He smiled and placed his credit card on the counter.

Max accepted Tom's outstretched hand with a firm grasp in a welcoming handshake. After they exchanged a few pleasantries, Tom took himself off to the nether regions of the store.

Katie began to ring him up. "You know, I found that the *three* fifty-foot hoses that are already at the station were plenty sufficient for any need that could arise."

"Did you? And how would you know that?" he drawled as he signed the ticket.

Katie's hackles started to rise. "Well, I did take care of the houses and the grounds for quite some time, doing things like watering the trees, the shrubs, and the flowerbeds, and cleaning the windows."

"Really? I was actually planning to hire someone to do that. You got any interest?" His lips quirked, revealing a crooked smile that pulled endearingly at the corners of his mouth.

Katie's lips clamped shut. Then taking a deep steadying breath, gave him a look that said *drop dead*. "No, I do not."

"I wondered, since you seemed hell bent on working there yesterday."

"Well, that was yesterday."

Then after a moment of silence as she waited for the

credit card to go through, she added, "You know if you're going to be replacing things, I would suggest the ladder. As you noticed yourself, it's terribly rickety, unsafe as a matter of fact."

He looked up from signing the ticket, suddenly changing the tone of the conversation, his eyes becoming more serious. "How are you, Katie?"

Caught off guard by his sincerity, Katie lowered her gaze from his as she pretended to busy herself with some papers on the counter.

"I was worried about you after you left last night."

He took her chin between his fingers, forcing her to meet his gaze. She raised her eyes to his briefly, then lowered them to stare at his shirt collar.

"Look at me." He spoke softly but with a firmness that commanded her attention, and she found herself unable to disobey.

She could drown in those gold-flecked eyes. Fighting it with every fiber of her being, she pulled her chin out of his lean fingers and said, "I'm perfectly fine, Mr. Sawyer. But we're closed now so if you don't mind, I have to balance the cash drawer."

Max Sawyer clenched his jaw, hardening his handsome features. "Thanks for the hoses." He strode out of the store, his words still reverberating against her eardrums.

## Chapter 5

"So let me get this straight. You're on your bike, you're practically run over by two cars, thrown into a ditch, and it was Max Sawyer who rescued you?" Jill asked with sparkle-eyed interest.

"I would hardly call it a rescue. He almost broke my arm." Katie took the tea glass from Jill's hand. "And get that smile off your face. I'll stick to chivalrous and charming if you don't mind."

"Oh, that sounds exciting," Jill stated with sarcasm, and shook her head at her friend. "Your problem is that you compare everyone you meet with that military guy you all but conjured up over the years. Your expectations are unrealistic. Really, how anyone could come up to such high standards is beyond me."

Placing the glasses in the sink, Katie turned back to Jill, arms folded across her chest. "Is that what you think? That I've conjured him up?"

"Oh, I think he's real enough, but you have fantasized about him to the point that there isn't much of a *man* left, if you follow?"

Katie leaned against the counter and sighed heavily. "So have you found out anything about Max?" she said, changing the subject.

"Only confirming that he develops historic properties," Jill said.

"Maybe he's going to actually restore it. You know, back to its former glory."

"I don't know, Sherlock. But, I'll keep you posted."

After Jill left, Katie picked up an apple, then headed down the back steps of her apartment, with Buddy at her heels. The afternoon sun cast ribbons of orange over the horizon making the water dance in the distance. It was only a short walk to the lighthouse. In minutes, her feet padded across the wide plank boards of the pier that led out over the water. Katie lowered herself in one lithe movement. Buddy plopped down beside her as her legs dangled over the edge. Swinging them back and forth, she bit into the green flesh of the Granny Smith apple, periodically wiping the juice from her chin with the back of her hand. She couldn't help herself and found her eyes straying to the two gray clapboard structures that sat quietly nearby. She shouldn't be here. Those beloved buildings belonged to him now. At least the tower wasn't his. Thoughts of the tower always led to thoughts of her sailor and most recently to Jill's comments. *Have I built him up in my mind until he's not even human anymore?*

Katie pitched the apple core into the water and sprinted across the green grass to the tower. She pulled open the door and ran up the iron steps that coiled in dizzying momentum with each step she took. Out of breath, she stopped abruptly at her and her sailor's spot, slid to the floor and leaned her right shoulder against the wall. She lifted her hand and with her index finger, carefully traced the slightly faded but still visible heart that lovingly embraced their initials.

"Are you real, or have I made you up?"

Katie gazed at the heart for several more seconds, then stood, turned, and careened into a powerful rock-hard chest. Steadying hands quickly caught hold of her, then just as quickly let her go.

"Well, hello. Are you the keeper?" Max's eyes held a slightly teasing glint.

A wary alertness came over her. *H*e certainly wasn't a phantom.

"Sorry to bother you, but I found"—One long-fingered hand flipped over the dog tag—"Buddy wandering around outside like he owned the place."

"Yes, well ... we come here a lot," she said as she curled her fingers around the bottom of her shirt. "What are you doing here?" She told herself that the sharpness in her voice was due to the fact that he had startled her, not to the fact his presence had somehow spoiled the moment. She pushed back the uncomfortable thought that he might have actually heard her talking to the wall.

One of his thick eyebrows rose. "Was I interrupting something?"

"No. It's just that no one hardly ever comes up here, and ..." Katie stopped, suddenly at a loss for words.

"I find that hard to believe. I imagine the view is quite beautiful."

Something about the way he was looking at her had her heart hammering in her chest. Suddenly, she was acutely aware that they were quite alone in the top of the narrow tower, with walls so thick that it would drown out all sound to the outside world.

"You startled me, that's all." She made a move to pass him.

"What's this?" he asked, pointedly looking at the heart on the wall behind her.

Katie stepped in front of it, unable to mask her irritation.

Undaunted, he peered over her shoulder. "Looks like I'm on your heart." Then he slowly raked his eyes over her body, causing her to take an involuntary step backward.

"W—what do you mean?"

An amused light entered his eyes at her small step of retreat. "My initials, they're on your heart."

"Trust me, they're not your initials."

He stepped around her for a better view. "Hum, M. S. If not me, then who?" He gave her a look that held a combination of curiosity and amusement.

"No one you know."

A slow grin spread across his features and his lips quirked into an irresistible smile. Her heart somersaulted like it was trying out for the Olympic gymnastic team.

"Belligerent. I certainly wouldn't have thought that of you." He folded his arms across his chest.

"Oh, I'm much more than that," she said, pushing a wayward gold strand behind her ear in irritation.

"Hum, you could be right." A twinkle appeared in his tawny eyes. "I'd say that's quite a few years ago," he said, his attention now back on the heart. "Anyone special?"

"At the time." She wondered what business it was of his anyway.

"I'll bet you were just a kid then. Fifteen or sixteen at the most." When she didn't answer, he continued. "That would make you a whopping twenty-something now, wouldn't it?"

Katie fought against succumbing to his charms. "I really don't see what my age has to do with anything. Look, is there a point to this? I *really* have to go now, so if you—"

"Let me guess," he interrupted, "first kiss?" His deep-set eyes mocked her as his lips formed a half smile that baited her.

The nerve of this guy.

"You know, just looking at you, I'd swear that you've never really been *properly* kissed before."

Her mouth fell open at that. "I have so been properly kissed," she insisted, hating that she was rising to the bait.

A raised brow framed the mocking light in his eyes. "By him, I suppose?" He motioned in the direction of the fading heart.

"That is none of your business. And just what do you mean by how I look? How is one supposed to look?"

"Well, certainly not like you with those big apprehensive eyes of yours. I'll bet you he was, what, sixteen or seventeen at the most?" He took a step toward her. "A boy's kiss, not even close to proper."

Katie, suddenly uncomfortable with where this conversation was heading, took a wobbly step backward. "Don't even think about it."

"Oh, I'm more than thinking about it," came the suave reply. "Your mouth is spouting one thing, but your eyes ..." He paused, allowing her to fill in the rest.

Katie could almost hear her heart pounding in her chest. Oh, God, she wanted him to kiss her. She wanted to know what it felt like to be really, truly and properly kissed.

As was the case when she was in a quandary, Katie's teeth clamped onto her bottom lip. She was hardly aware that he'd stepped closer until he raised his hand to her chin. With his thumb, he gently pulled her bottom lip from between her teeth. He lowered his head. Her heart fluttered like a wild bird in her chest, and her trembling body became rigid, poised to flee.

Pulling her closer, Max kissed her. His lips moved over hers with sweet persuasion, demanding in its very tenderness, a response from her. Katie saw stars, and swayed toward him. Tingling, wonderful warmth invaded her entire being. She quivered with both fear and anticipation as her arms tentatively reached around his waist, surrendering to the feel of him. He smelled wonderful, like citrus and fresh woods. His lips left hers and moved to the side of her mouth. She breathed in deeply to remember his scent.

"Was that proper enough for you?" he asked, his voice husky against her ear.

Katie's eyes flew open. A wave of cold water couldn't have hit her any harder. He was laughing at her. Her trembling hands pushed hard against his chest so much that she almost toppled over.

"You're despicable," she hissed.

"Not exactly the response I was expecting," he stated

as he leaned back against the rail, his brown eyes suddenly sharp and direct. Waiting. Watching.

Then straightening, he placed his fingers to his forehead in a mock salute and clipped down the stairs.

Fuming at being laughed at, Katie turned on Buddy. "Some guard dog you turned out to be."

Katie stared at the heart on the wall. It seemed to mock her as well. An intense longing welled up inside of her that felt familiar, yet not. She tried to hold on to it, for it seemed to be trying to escape from somewhere back in her memory, but just as quickly, it disappeared, leaving a wake of frustration in her heart. Tenderly, she reached out toward the heart and traced the M and then the S repeating his name, Max Sawyer, as she did so. Then she whispered the words the initials actually stood for ... my sailor." For just a moment, Katie let her imagination run wild. Bewildered, she shook her head and made her way down the steps.

Max shut the door of his Z4 and started the engine. His heart was racing from sheer exhilaration. He could still see her standing in the narrow confines of the tower, tall and lovely in her white short-shorts, her long legs poised for flight. His pulse quickened at the thought of her soft curves. He'd wanted to pull that blue ribbon from her hair and watch it tumble over her shoulders. He'd wanted to go on kissing her, but he could tell he'd lit the fight or flight response in her. Although, he didn't want a fight, as interesting as that might have been some other time, neither did he want the latter response. His chest tightened, as he thought of the longing openly displayed in her blue eyes.

Was she really such an innocent? Innocence coupled with her spirit was a heady combination. That young woman was death to a man's freedom, and she didn't even realize it.

## Chapter 6

The next day, after class, Katie boarded the ferry to return to town.

"Miss McCullough." The scruffy-bearded captain of *The Talbot* tipped his hat to her as he did to all his regulars. As the ferry left the dock, a gust of wind shot across the bow, causing her to grab the rail for support. The wind blew unusually strong, whipping her curls across her face. Without thought, she lifted a hand to push the offending strands out of her eyes and watched as they slid by Paige Point Lighthouse. Katie shook her head and scoffed inwardly at her naïve, romantic notions. *Like he would really show up after all these years.*

Deeply inhaling the salty air, Katie came to a decision. She would drop this semester. She needed time to sort out her life. Plus, the extra hours would enable her to finish the paintings for Falcon Designs. Thinking of Falcon, she quickly checked her phone, but still no message. Thirty minutes later, she found herself staring at the front door of her aunt's two-story Victorian home.

She entered, discovering it was still as dark inside as she remembered, with thick drapes at all the windows. With an impulsive movement, she yanked and tugged until the drapes fell to the floor, sending up a wave of dust that had her coughing uncontrollably. Slapping at the dust, she ran over to the next window and ripped down that massive length of fabric as well. Sunlight flooded through the glass panes, enveloping her with its sparkling warmth. As she surveyed the place, her spirits lifted. The light was not only therapeutic, but also symbolic with the washing away of her aunt's rigid and controlling nature and haunting memories of her childhood. She and Pop would live here.

An hour later, Katie waved to the receptionist as she went in the retirement home, then took the short hallway to Pop's apartment. She burst into his compact living room. "Pop, Pop, I've figured out what we need to do."

"Katie, darlin'."

"We're going to move into Aunt Margaret's house," she announced grandly.

"But you hate Margaret's house."

"It doesn't matter about that. I've got it all worked out. Besides, you can't keep living here."

"Exactly what I've been telling him."

Katie whipped around at the sound of Max's voice. "What are you doing here?"

"Katie, Max is my guest." Pop sounded a bit embarrassed.

"It's all right, Angus. I'm afraid Katie and I got off to a rocky start."

*So it's Angus, is it?* "What does he mean, Pop? What's going on?"

"Max and I have had a nice discussion. He has invited me to come live at the light station, and I'm seriously considering it. He's doing research on the lighthouse and since I'm familiar with much of its history, he wants my help."

"What?"

"Angus has a wealth of information about Page Point, and as I intend to restore it, I thought he could be of great service to me. Frankly, I thought you'd be pleased."

"Mr. Sawyer," Katie said in a business-like tone, trying to get control of her emotions, "I ... of course it's a very nice gesture, but I intend for Pop to live with me." She stood before him, rigid with frustration and suspicion.

Max's cell phone rang, breaking the tense atmosphere. "Excuse me, this is the call I was expecting, Angus." Max strode into the next room to take it.

"Pop, you haven't told him anything, have you?" she whispered. "About me, and the light station?"

"Of course not, but I don't understand all this secrecy."

"Please, Pop. Not a word."

Pop raised a gnarled hand to her. Katie took it and stood close to his chair, deliberately turning her back toward the direction Max had disappeared.

"I know how long you've tried to make things work out for us to be together," Pop said in a quiet voice. He placed his other hand over hers. "You don't really want to live in Margaret's house. I know you don't. Besides, if I'm living at the light station, I bet he'd let you use the oil house as your studio. I know how much you love the place." Pop gave Katie a subtle wink.

"Oh, Pop," Katie said softly. He had no idea. She'd had it all worked out, until Max Sawyer had come along to ruin it all. She slid to her knees beside his chair. "Pop, you're my family. Please don't move in with him."

"You could come, too."

"No, I could never live there now."

Pop held up a feeble hand, putting a stop to Katie's outburst. "Nothing has been decided yet. Now, I want you to be nice to my guest while I fix you some tea."

Katie slowly got to her feet and silently watched as he made his way to the kitchen. She turned, surprised to see that Max had already returned from the other room and stood leaning against the doorframe.

Frustrated at seeing him standing there like he owned the place, she blurted out, "Who are you? What do you want? Why are you taking everything from me?"

"Whoa ... slow down, angel. I've already told you who I am. As for what I want, well, I'm still working on that." He offered a devilish grin. "And just how have I taken everything from you by offering a kindly old man a home? Which frankly is more than you've been able to do. As a matter of fact, before you burst in ..."

"How dare you say such a thing to me?"

"Look, it's obvious you care deeply for him and that you'd like to see him out of this stale place. As I'm sure he's a man who would not accept charity, I have just provided him with a way to do that. You of all people must see that."

"Of course I see that," she spat out, her voice low, aware of Pop in the next room.

"You should be happy for him. Instead you're letting your obvious dislike for me keep him from what surely would be a blessing and a gift. In a matter of two days, I've been able to accomplish what you haven't been able to do in, what did I hear him say, two years?"

Heat flashed to her face. "That's a low blow," she said. "I didn't know you were the type to hit below the belt."

"Since when is the truth hitting below the belt? I'm not saying your intentions weren't good, just that your methods have failed."

Katie felt the color drain from her face. The nerve of this man. "So, what will you do after you have all of your historical information, put him out on the street?"

Max's jaw tightened. "Let me assure you, I would never put Angus 'out on the street.'"

Katie dropped her eyes away from his piercing ones. "This home has a waiting list you know. There is no guarantee that he could even get back in here."

"Maybe by then something else may have been worked out. This project of mine will take several months to complete. You might even have your plans worked out by then, and he could still move in with you."

"It must be so nice to be rolling in money," she said with all the haughty disdain she could muster.

"You have something against money?"

"Only when it's used in place of hard work and ingenuity." She watched his jaw tighten. "Do you always just buy what you want, Mr. Sawyer?"

"Sometimes, but not always. There are other ways of acquiring what one wants," he said softly. "Why is it so important for you to take care of him?"

"He's like a grandfather to me. He practically raised me. My brother and I lived with him for years, and I feel a responsibility toward him, just as any granddaughter would. I don't know what sort of game you're playing at, Mr. Sawyer, but rest assured, I will find out."

"A little respect and a lot less belligerence would go a long way with me."

"Well, don't expect it from me any time soon. You may be master and commander of all you survey and you may even get him to do your bidding,"—she threw out her hand toward the kitchen—"but to me, you're nothing but a thief."

Max's arm snaked out and jerked her to his strong frame. "If I were you, I'd be careful with that impetuous little mouth of yours. I bid on that property fair and square, just like anyone else could have done. I'm sorry the timing didn't suit you. You ever call me a thief again, and I'll see you in court." With that, he let go of her arm.

"You don't like the truth, so you think you can just threaten me?"

"Angel, that was no threat."

Fury surged like a tidal wave. She pointed a slender finger toward the kitchen. "Well, you'd better not do anything to hurt him or you'll have me to answer to." She jabbed her finger into his chest. "There are ways of dealing with people like you, and you will not harm Pop." With that, she stormed out of the room and out of the home.

Katie drove to the light station fighting mad. "*I* wouldn't take anything from Max Sawyer if he were the last chance on earth. If Pop wants to live with him, then he can." Still fuming, she all but threw her supplies from the oil house into her vehicle.

Reason began to take hold as she drove over to her aunt's. She'd made a complete fool of herself. What was wrong with her? She'd acted like some blasted yappy little dog with Max. Okay, so maybe Max was trying to be helpful, but did he have to be so completely, overbearingly male about everything? Next time, she'd be polite and in control.

Katie parked in the back, unloaded the vehicle, then entered the house. She threw herself into one of the living room chairs to catch her breath. As she sat there, her thoughts traveled back to another time she had been in this room. It was the evening of Davy's funeral. She had just come back from the lighthouse and had walked through every room looking for *him*. Craning her neck above and around the guests, she finally saw her sailor at the front entrance. He was just leaving, and even though his back was to her, she knew it was him. Her eyes locked onto his uniformed shoulders and she watched as her sailor walked out the door. That's how she had come to think of him over the years, as her sailor. If only she had run after him then, she might have been able to see his face. If only. The memory of him was so dear to her. His dress blues, his masculine wrists cuffed in crisp white, brass-studded cufflinks that sparkled through her tears. She remembered fully how she had wept against him, in the darkness of the tower, clutching the lapels of his coat, heedless of the imprint of the buttons on her face.

Katie got up from the chair and with a deep sigh carried the box of art supplies to a corner bedroom and set up her studio. Setting up was easy, and in no time she'd completed blocking out a new painting.

Needing a break, she went to the kitchen and opened

the door to a large pantry. Nothing had changed here. The teabags sat right where they'd always been. In minutes, the kettle was singing, and with a hot cup of tea in her hand, she made her way to the widow's walk located on top of the house. She stood staring out toward the horizon, as had the women of long ago, waiting for their men to return from months at sea. She leaned into the rail, cradling the warm cup in her hands, her mind deep in thought. It would take some time to make this house a studio and a home, but she could do it. But first she had a score to settle with Mr. Max Sawyer.

## Chapter 7

For the first time in many months, Katie spent the night in her Aunt Margaret's house. She had worked well into the evening on her watercolor and was pleased with what she'd accomplished. That *creative something* had moved within her, compelling her to paint late into the night. Falling asleep in her old room had turned out to be easier than she'd thought it would be. Crawling into her old bed, she was asleep as soon as her head hit the pillow. She woke up the next morning to the sound of a lawn mower, stretched, and let Buddy out the back door into the fenced in back yard. Yawning, she realized how relaxed she felt. Something had happened yesterday. She would be hard-pressed to explain it, but she knew she had gone through some sort of healing process. Maybe ripping the draperies off the windows had been more than the symbolic gesture she had first thought.

Katie stepped back from her watercolor, a slow smile spreading across her features. *It's good, the best I've ever done.*

"One down and five more to go," she told Buddy. His tail thumped on the floor at the sound of her voice. Katie reached for her cell phone and scrolled through her contacts for the number for Falcon Designs and Sally Batson. Finding it, she pressed 'send.'

"Hello," the pleasant voice of a young man said on the other end of the line.

"Yes, hello, this is Katie McCullough, and I'd like to

speak to Sally Batson, please."

"She's not available right now. Would you like to leave a message?"

"Yes, please. Would you have her call Katie McCullough?" Katie spelled out her name, then proceeded to give him her phone number.

"I'll see that she gets this."

"Thank you." Katie snapped her phone shut with an odd feeling that she was being avoided.

Friday morning, the ringing of Katie's cell phone dragged her from a deep sleep. "Okay, okay, I hear you." She pulled herself up to a sitting position while reaching out for the phone. Glancing at the caller ID, she saw Lily's name on the screen.

"Lily, hey," Katie answered, stifling a yawn.

"Hey, Katie, just checking in with you. I noticed you didn't come back the last couple of nights, and I wanted to make sure you were all right."

"I'm fine, Lily. Believe it or not, I'm at Aunt Margaret's. I've set up one of the bedrooms as a studio and have completed my first watercolor for Falcon. I worked so late that I just spent the night."

"So, you've heard from them then?"

"No, but I did call and leave a message for Miss Batson to call me back. So we'll see."

"Are you sure you're all right staying there?" Lily asked with a tinge of concern in her voice.

"Yes, I can hardly believe it myself. I think I'm going to stay tonight, too. I'm on a roll with these paintings, so I'll probably spend a few more days here. Hey, will you guys be at the park tonight?"

"Of course, we wouldn't dare miss the last Movie in

the Park night. Remember, whoever gets there first saves the spot."

Max sat at the sleek glass and maple desk in his corner office that overlooked the quintessential eastern shore town of St. Michaels. The space was covered with natural light, adding spectacular warmth to the comfortable seating area. His assistant, Sally Batson, sat across from him with coffee in hand to discuss the Markesan hotel project.

"Okay, Sal, what have you got?"

"We have one week before we give Peter and his board the design presentation," she said.

"So how are you coming on finding this girl? Her drawings are fabulous." He flipped through the composite she had left behind.

"Still no luck, boss. I was only with her for a few minutes before I went to get Fred. I still can't believe she would walk out, leaving her sketches behind, but no way for us to contact her? She hasn't even tried to contact us. I don't get it."

Max leaned forward, placed his elbows on the desk, and continued to leaf through the drawings.

"I feel terrible, Max. I only went to get Fred because of my blasted allergies. I was having one of my sneezing fits when I left the room. I'd only left for a moment—"

Max raised his right hand, stopping her in mid sentence. "I know. It's not your fault." Max rubbed his hand through his hair.

"I've already checked with the art magazine who did the feature on her," Sal continued, "but they can't give us her personal information because of confidentiality laws."

"Can't they contact her like they did before?"

"They tried, but apparently, she's no longer at that address."

"Nothing, not even a phone number?"

Sally shook her head.

Max leaned back in his leather chair, tapping his Mont Blanc fountain pen in the palm of his left hand. "Katherine Clare, where the heck are you?"

"Peter has already signed off on these on my word, no less. If we can't deliver, we could lose this account and you know how much that's worth." He let out a heavy, disgruntled sigh, and tossed his pen on the black pad lying on his desk. "There's no more time. We have to find another artist. What about Alan Parker? As I recall, he's both talented and fast. And right now, we need both."

"Actually, that's who I was going to suggest until I saw this girl's work."

"Ok, just give Alan the particulars, but not how we intend to use his work. That way if we find this Katherine Clare, we can use Alan's paintings on another project. In the meantime, I'll work on getting an extension from Peter on the art. We have everything else lined up for the rest of the project, don't we?"

"Yes, our only holdup is the original art for the lobbies."

"All right, keep me posted," Max said as he stood to leave.

"Another appointment, boss?"

"Yes, to catch the *Talbot* back to Page Point."


Arriving a little earlier than normal, Katie parked her Jeep along the side street closest to the park. Since this was the last Movie in the Park for the year, there would be a huge turnout. She circled the vehicle, careful not to let any dirt get on her navy Capri pants and her white blouse that hung untucked from beneath her green sweater. She reached in the back and removed the lawn chair, blanket, and picnic basket. Bessie usually brought loads of food so between hers and the

Jeffrey's they would enjoy quite a feast.

Katie claimed a nice, slightly sloping area about halfway back from the screen and spread out her blanket. She noticed plenty of people already milling around, checking out the sale booths and grabbing their spot for the movie.

"Need any help?" Max asked, his deep voice now very familiar.

"Mr. Sawyer." Startled, Katie stood there holding her foldout chair up off the ground, wondering who had invited him.

"So you're still insisting on this ridiculous formality, huh?" He took the chair out of her hands, unfolded it, and placed it on the grass next to the blanket. "This spot okay?"

She nodded, suddenly feeling awkward in his presence. Since she swore to be polite the next time she saw him, she asked, "Would you ... like to join us?"

"Careful. Don't choke on those words."

She couldn't help it. Her lips twitched and she strangely found herself warming to him.

"Amazing."

"What?" she asked, tentatively.

"You almost smiled at me," he said, catching her off guard. "I was beginning to wonder if your scowl was permanent or if it was only reserved for me." His smile was sheer devastation. He was, without doubt, the most gorgeous man she had ever seen. Suddenly, she felt an inward pull toward him, like a float on a wave being brought to shore. Buoyant, but helpless. Stunned by her reaction, she immediately put up a wall in a vain attempt to shut him out. He was a thief, an intruder. The home she'd always wanted was gone because of him, and nothing could ever change that.

"Hello, there."

Katie and Max turned as Bessie's ample figure approached them. Pop's rangy lean form was one step behind, carrying the chairs. Bessie spread her blanket next to Katie's and set her large basket of food on top. Max took one of the chairs from Angus and proceeded to set them up in a slight arch so they could visit as well as see the movie screen.

"Glad to see you could make it, son." Angus reached out to shake Max's outstretched hand.

"I wouldn't have missed it," Max said with a pleasant smile.

Katie's heart sank. So Pop had invited him. As she watched the two men, she was struck by how well they seemed to get along. In such a short period of time, there was a poignant familiarity between them. A rapport that usually took months, if not years, to develop.

Katie turned her back on them. A chilling hand gripped her heart. Would she lose Pop to the charms of this outsider? She knew it was selfish on her part, but she couldn't deny the pain this caused her.

"Earth to Katie."

Jill, her parents, and her little brother were standing in her midst, and she hadn't even been aware of it.

"Where were you?" Jill teased, eyes alight with laughter.

Shaking her head, Katie focused on Jill and her family. The Jeffreys were a great family. Jill's parents, Miles and Mary, now in their late forties, had been surprised by Jill's little brother, Jamey, nine plus years ago, as they thought they could never have any more children. This unexpected addition to the family had been met with great joy. Jill completely doted on her little brother and he of course adored her, too.

Folks had now come out in mass. The park hummed with activity. The band started to play while Frisbees sailed through the air amidst smiles and laughter.

The women in their little group soon had the banquet spread before them and called to the guys who were nearby playing soccer. Pop had actually joined in, albeit just to cheer on little Jamey. As he approached the group, he grabbed hold of Bessie's arm and led her to a chair.

"Pop and Bessie are so cute. Do they always act like that when they're together?" Jill whispered to Katie.

"Of course not." Katie looked at Jill as if she'd grown another head.

"I don't know ... looks like he's courting her to me."

"Oh, Pop always acts like that."

Eventually, they all sat back pretty well stuffed. Miles, without asking, pulled his wife of twenty-three years laughingly to her feet and dragged her over to the makeshift dance platform near the band. Katie and Jill began helping Bessie with the cleanup, but she waved them away with her plump hands and told them to go enjoy themselves. At that moment, Katie looked up to see Max's eyes on her, and she knew he was going to ask her to dance. Something close to terror welled up inside of her. As she searched frantically for a way out, Jamey suddenly stood before her tugging insistently on her arm. With immense relief, Katie followed him to the platform, but not before she caught the amused expression on Max's face.

As soon as they stepped foot on the wood planks, the band struck up the old Stevie Wonder song, "Isn't She Lovely?" Katie, totally relaxed with her young partner, twisted and turned in rhythm to the music. Laughing, Jamey held her hands as she spun him into her swaying body, then back out, allowing him to spin her toward his small frame in turn.

"Katie, will you marry me?" Jamey asked, breathless as he moved about on the wooden floor.

Katie smiled down into his glowing little face. "Wow, marriage. That's pretty serious stuff. I'll tell you what, how about we go out on a date first?"

Jamey's face lit up as he responded with a resounding, "Yea, that'd be great! When?"

"Soon."

"Pinky promise?"

"You bet."

Max watched them twirling with a slight smile playing about his lips while he leaned comfortably against one of the park's many oak trees.

Jill approached, an encouraging smile across her glossy lips. "You can get a lot closer if we go out there, you know. You like her."

"Of course I like her," he replied with a matter-of-fact lift of his shoulders.

"No, I mean you *like* her."

"So you think I need help?"

"Oh, not with Katie. I'm sure if you want to, you can have her in the palm of your hand. It's my little brother you'll need help with. If you try to break in on them, he'll flat tell you no."

"So what do you suggest?"

"Just leave it to me," she said, then took him by the arm and led him onto the platform.

As they stepped up on the boards, the band hit the final chords, then expertly led into another number. This one happened to be slow. Before Jamey could take Katie into his little arms, Jill, with Max in tow, pushed her way through the crowd and then held out her arms to her little brother. "This is my favorite." She smiled lovingly down at Jamey's freckled face. That's all it took. He relinquished Katie in a flash and happily paired off with his sister.

Before Katie knew what happened, Max had her in his arms, ignoring her obvious resistance. She went rigid, fearing he would pull her closer to him.

"Relax, will you?"

"I really don't feel like dancing," Katie said, suddenly nervous.

"Well, it looked like you were having an awfully good time dancing a few moments ago. So, I guess that means you don't feel like dancing with me."

"Look, I don't mean to sound rude, but I'd just like to sit this one out." Katie glanced up at him. For an answer, Max pulled her a bit closer to his rugged frame. The strength of him, his nearness as his left hand splayed against her back, left her breathless. He held her in a secure grip that allowed him to guide her smoothly across the wide planks under their feet. Katie felt tense and on alert. Her legs grew weak and shaky. Seconds later, she stumbled, allowing Max to maneuver her tightly against him. The warmth in his eyes was almost her undoing, so Katie dropped her gaze to his collarbone. In a rising panic, her heart quickened a beat. Suddenly breathless, it took all of her concentration to keep up with him. She tried to tell herself that it must be the anxiety from the past few weeks, but as soon as she thought it, she knew it was a lie.

"I have a proposition for you," Max said, interrupting her thoughts.

Katie's gaze flew up to meet his.

"I want you to move into the keeper's house."

She bristled and held herself even more rigid in his arms.

"With Angus," he clarified, a definite glint of mockery now evident in his eyes. "You realize he won't come because of you. He's informed me he won't move in unless you do."

*So he only wants me in order to get him.* A fleeting wave of disappointment washed over her, taking her by complete surprise. "Look, I appreciate what you're trying to do."

"Do you? I want you to go by and see him tonight and

take a good long look at his surroundings and tell me he wouldn't be better off at the light station."

She stared him full in the face. "I know what his surroundings look like. That's the second time you've thrown that in my face," she said through clenched teeth.

"Look, I'm sorry if I spoke out of turn. But I run two businesses and my hours are crazy. It would make things a lot easier if Angus just moved in to help me. He'll come if you come, Katie."

"I'm sorry, but Pop is going to live with me, and that's final."

"And how many years from now will that be? And where do you plan on living? Your Aunt Margaret's house? That monstrosity will take more money than you have for the two of you to live in it for any length of time, and you know it. And how do you plan to pay the bills with a part-time job? A house that size will have you drained in months."

He was absolutely right, yet how did he know about her financial situation? Of course, being Mr. Moneybags, he would be able to guess because of her age and obvious lack of resources. But how could he possibly know how big her aunt's house was?

The dance came to an end. Max took her elbow and walked her back to the lawn chairs. Then he smiled his devastating smile toward Mary and asked if she would like to dance. Mary went off happily with her escort, and Katie found herself sitting alone. Jill was some distance away chatting with some of her friends and Bessie and Pop were strolling through the craft booths. Miles and Jamey were off somewhere as well, so Katie decided to cut the cake and had the slices ready and waiting for their return. That done, she sat down, then checked her phone for messages. Nothing. Everyone showed up in good spirits at about the same time and dove in to the thick slices of strawberry cake.

"Where are Tom and Lily?" Bessie asked. "I thought

sure they'd be here tonight?"

"I got a message from her. Tom's sick so they won't be coming."

"That means you'll be working at R and R tomorrow," Jill said.

"R and R," Jamey said, licking icing off his fingers. "What does that mean, Jill?"

"Rods n' Reels." She smiled back at him, ruffling his hair.

"What does she mean you'll be working tomorrow? Don't you have classes?" Pop asked, his blue eyes bright as they looked across at her.

Katie had just taken a bite of cake. With her mouth full, she could only look back at him, then over at Jill, who looked back at her with a contrite expression on her round face. Katie chewed slowly, her mind groping for an answer. She was completely embarrassed that Max was witnessing her discomfiture. She swallowed convulsively. "Pop, I'm taking the semester off. I'm sorry, I just haven't had a chance to tell you." She gave him a look of mute appeal for him not to talk about it in front of everybody, but he either ignored it or he didn't understand.

"Your life is your own, Katie, darlin', as I've been telling you. You've always made good decisions. I'm not worried about you, especially if you only plan to take this semester off. There are worst things, to be sure."

She nodded, thankful the show was about to start.

The movie that night was the old Cole Porter musical, *Kiss Me, Kate.*

"Hey, Katie, she has the same name as you," Jamey said, pointing out the obvious with wide–eyed amazement.

"Wasn't this movie based on Shakespeare's *The Taming of the Shrew*?" Jill asked, looking around at the entire group now seated comfortably in lawn chairs.

"Yes, it was," her dad answered.

"I just love Cole Porter's music," Bessie chimed in.

Jamey, having found a new friend in Max asked innocently, "What's a shrew?"

Katie, who was sitting on the other side of Jamey, found herself straining to hear Max's answer. "Well, in this case, it's a young lady who is highly opinionated, impulsive, headstrong, willful, stubborn, *and* obstinate."

Katie looked over at him and found to her annoyance that he was looking right at her with a mocking gleam in his eyes. Katie raised her chin.

"Oh, and let's not forget defiant," Max added as his head leaned toward Jamey's in a conspiratorial manner.

"She sounds real bratty to me." Jamey's nose wrinkled in strong disapproval.

"Exactly," Max agreed, then bumped fists with Jamey.

"But not like *our* Katie," Jamey stated emphatically.

Katie rolled her eyes heavenward, slumped down in her chair, and folded her arms across the front of her sweater. Near the end, when the character Petruchio spanks Katherina, Jamey clapped enthusiastically. "She sure deserved that, don't you think, Katie?"

"Well," she hesitated, and before she could say anything else, Max chimed in.

"Yes, Katie, tell us what you think?"

Katie drew in a sharp breath and scowled at Max across the top of Jamey's head. "I think he was a despicable brute who lost control of himself as well as his temper. Any man who has to resort to physical violence isn't a gentleman."

Jamey frowned, clearly not happy with Katie's answer.

"So, Katie, how should a man deal with a woman who is willful, obstinate, and a troublemaker?"

*He should tell her he loves her and kiss her to distraction.* The thought jumped unbidden into Katie's mind, startling her. But when she looked up to see the mocking gleam in Max's eyes, she was brought back to reality with a jolt. "Remember, Jamey, there are gentleman and there are *pigs.*"

"Pigs? What do pigs have to do with it?" he asked, clearly confused.

Katie closed her eyes before letting out a sigh that clearly said this conversation had gotten out of hand. She put her fingers to her lips in a quieting gesture. "Nothing, sweetheart. Let's finish the movie, shall we?"

"Oh look, they're kissing, yuck!" a clearly disgusted Jamey loudly exclaimed, causing a burst of laughter from their little group.

## Chapter 8

The next day, Katie's cell rang out from the phone-charger that was plugged in at the kitchen counter. She knew from the ring tone it was Jill calling. She hastily laid her sable watercolor brush down next to her art pad. Jumping up from her swivel chair, she almost tripped over Buddy's sprawled form lying at her feet. "Sorry, boy," she managed to get out as she answered the phone.

"Hello, Watson. Did you find anything else?"

"More of the same actually, but with a twist. I think you'll find what I've discovered very interesting."

"Shoot."

"Not yet. This is too good to reveal over the phone. I'll be right over."

"I'm at Aunt Margaret's."

"You're kidding."

"No, I'm not, and if you don't get your little self over here, I'll—"

"Already in the car, honey."

When Jill arrived, she sat down, crossed her legs, then leaned back, spreading both arms over the back of the green sofa. Katie plopped down across from her and curled up in the green-and-yellow upholstered chair.

Jill surveyed the room. "I like what you've done with the place, lots of light."

"Jill!" Katie snapped.

"Your Mr. Sawyer is in the hotel business," Jill said, her warm brown eyes aglow with a look that clearly revealed she was savoring this moment.

"So? You couldn't tell me this over the phone? As I recall, he's also a developer, so this connection is not unusual."

"There's more. His particular specialty is turning quaint historic buildings into small, but luxurious five-star inns." Jill paused for effect, then with a smile that resembled the Cheshire cat's continued. "And his most recent finished project in that line is a light station including the lighthouse."

Katie's heart sank and she felt her eyes grow wide. "He wouldn't."

"I think he already is. Haven't you been by there lately? There's a large crew already working at the keeper's house."

"No, I haven't. I've been here painting." Katie jumped up and began pacing around the living room.

"I can see what you're thinking," Jill said calmly from the sofa. "Now don't go rushing over there like some wild woman until you look at the research I've gathered from the Internet. I brought it all with me." She took a folder from her purse and laid it on the coffee table in front of her.

Katie stopped pacing, sat down next to Jill, and picked up the material. "M.F.S. Enterprise specializes in luxurious yet intimate surroundings, set in beautifully restored historical settings. Experience exquisite culinary fare and divine pampering at our exclusive Serenity Spas. For the ultimate getaway, visit our website or call your local travel agent."

"Look, you have a lot to think about and I have to go. Some of us are still in school, you know," Jill said playfully.

"It all makes sense," Katie said as she walked Jill to the front door. "Did you know he's asked Pop to move onto the property to help with research? Can you believe the nerve of the guy? He waltzes in here, snatches a home away from a poor elderly man, then has the audacity to use him to further his own financial ends and then if that isn't enough, turn our beloved light station into some hoity-toity resort spa!"

"Oh, Katie." Jill laughed. "That's a little much even for you. Come on, you don't even know for sure that he's going to turn the station into an inn. You can't confront him with wild accusations until you're sure. You need to keep digging, find proof, and then you can have at him."

"Proof?" She slapped the pages. "This is all the proof I need."

Bits of oyster shell spewed out from under the tires of Katie's Jeep as it screeched to a halt. Without knocking, she stomped into the keeper's house to find Max working on an open windowsill on the bottom floor.

"So you're in the hotel business." Katie threw the sheaf of papers down on the table near where he was working.

"Yes and good afternoon to you, too." Max stopped for a brief moment, then continued to sand the windowsill. "I see you've been doing some research." His firm lips twitched.

"If you think you are going to turn this," she said, waving her arms through the air, "into one of your Serenity Spa Inns, then you are dreaming, Mister."

"Is that so?" Max straightened and his eyes locked with hers.

"You bet. I'll never let that happen."

His tawny eyes gave her a once over. "And you think you're big enough to stop me?"

"Yes," she spat out. "Don't think I can't. I'll rally the entire town if I have to. This is not what the council agreed to when they accepted your bid."

Max's brown eyes turned glacial. "Careful, angel. That sounds like a threat. If it is, you'll come off the worse for it."

Katie inhaled sharply. "You may have been master of all you commanded, but you won't master me."

Max stopped working and turned toward her. Even in her anger, Katie noticed his shirt, unbuttoned and clinging to his muscular form damp with the sweat of his labor, his forearms glistening with perspiration mingled with tiny particles of wood shavings.

"Maybe we should put that to the test?" he drawled.

"There's no maybe about it." Inhaling sharply, Katie gathered up her papers and stormed out of the house.

Saturday at four a.m., dressed completely in black, Katie reached into the pocket of her yoga pants, pulled out the duplicate key, and slid it into the lock. She turned the key until she heard the telltale click of the deadbolt retreating into the door. Slowly turning the handle, she held her breath, then gently pushed the heavy door open. Slipping into the cottage, she slid the backpack off her shoulders and placed it quietly on the floor. She removed the faucet handles from both of the bathroom sinks as well as the one in the kitchen. Carrying an armful of towels, she left the main bathroom, grinning at the surprise the *Master* would get in the morning. As quietly as possible, she removed the top and middle hinges from all of the doors except for the bedroom where he was sleeping.

She was tempted to remove the downstairs doorknobs as well, but they were original to the cottage so she left them. *I am not a thief. These are mine.* She quietly placed the handles and hinges in the backpack, then slung the heavy parcel through her arms before hoisting it over her shoulders. She crept slowly across the floor back to the front door, then paused to glance back over her shoulder at what was supposed to be her little home. With a grimace from the weight on her back, she stepped through the door and closed it quietly behind her. Round One complete. She crouched low as she scurried away. Her steps quickened, turning into a soft, but somewhat panicked, jog. Breathless from the fear of being discovered, Katie stopped and threw herself behind a bush. She flashed a grin of success at her partner in crime.

"I can't believe I'm helping you do this," Jill said, hefting another heavy bag. "This is breaking and entering."

"I just went in to get some of my things," Katie reasoned with smug satisfaction.

"We could get into a lot of trouble for this."

"Relax. That's why after tonight I'm going solo."

"Why after tonight?"

"I only needed you for moral support. And to carry a few things." She grinned. "Frankly, that was a breeze. The *Master* slept through the whole thing."

Shirtless and wearing lightweight cotton drawstring pants, Max stood by his bed and stretched. He stared out of the window at the sunlight dancing on the water, blinding in its brightness. He rubbed his hand back and forth through his blond crop of hair, then walked into the bathroom still half asleep. He reached out to turn on the faucet. His firm hands grabbed hold of ... nothing. "What the—?"

Moments later, he flushed the toilet and watched as the water rose to a threatening height. Suddenly wide awake, he held his breath, then quickly reached for a towel to deal with the impending overflow, only to find the towels no longer hanging on the bars. Frantically, he looked around for a plunger, but found no plunger, either. Jumping back as the water poured onto the tile floor, Max let out an expletive that would have shocked his mother. He yanked open the cabinet door and was pulled up short as he found it empty. He sprinted up the stairs and grabbed a handful of towels from there. Ten minutes later, four bath towels lay soaked on the floor. Fuming, he walked into the kitchen to make coffee. The sight of the empty space where the sink handles were supposed to be stopped him in his tracks.

Pulse pounding in his ears, he grabbed a bottle of filtered

water to wash his hands. Those formerly under his command knew well not to cross him. He'd left grown men quaking in their boots. So one annoying young woman should be no problem.

Katie sat on the floor of the hardware/tackle shop, stacking a lower shelf with supplies. As she methodically shifted boxes, she heard a pair of determined footsteps approaching her. She leaned to her side to look down the aisle and felt a sick feeling in the pit of her stomach. A pair of eyes that reminded Katie of a hawk seeking its prey pierced hers, and within seconds a pair of muscular legs stopped within inches of her sitting form.

His golden brown eyes pinned her to the floor, sending a chill down her spine. Outwardly, she strove to look as calm as she could. After all, she wasn't supposed to know why he was so angry. Slowly, deliberately he rolled up his sleeves like there was something symbolic in the gesture.

"May I help you?" she all but squeaked.

"Yes, as a matter of fact, you can. I need faucet handles. Bathroom and kitchen," he said in a clipped tone.

Katie stood and brushed at the back of her gray cords, then nervously tugged at her red cardigan.

"Over here," she said as she led him to the plumbing aisle.

"Oh dear, it seems we're out," Katie said in mock sorrow and slipped her booted foot toward the bottom shelf, making sure the box filled with faucet handles stayed hidden underneath.

His jaw clenched as he stared at the empty tray.

"Um, we could order them for you. It would only take a few days, a week at the most," she said, beginning to enjoy herself.

After a short detour, he followed her to the counter

where she commenced to look through the catalogue.

"Seems you're out of plungers as well," he said, clearly exasperated.

She found the pages with a variety of handles.

"Which ones would you like?"

Max jabbed one long finger onto the page in front of them, his steady glare never leaving her face.

"All right, how many?" She looked up at him with the most innocent expression she could muster and met his hostile glare. Shockwaves ran through her limbs at his expression. She realized she might have bitten off more then she could chew and wished she could spit some of it out.

Max took a deep, controlling breath. "Two sets of the bathroom size and one larger set for the kitchen."

"In which finish, nickel, brass or—"

"Chrome."

As she typed the order into the computer, she couldn't resist asking, "What's wrong with the handles that are already in the cottage?"

He smiled at her. "Who said these were for the cottage?"

Katie blinked up at him, her mind groping for a reasonable reply. "Well, I just assumed." She shrugged. "I wasn't aware you had another place?"

"You assumed right. These are for the cottage. It seems there's a thief in our quaint little fishing village."

"Really?" Her eyes widened in feigned surprise. "How terrible."

"It certainly is."

Something in his tone had her heart hammering in her breast.

"Have—have you reported it to the sheriff? We have had vandals in the area."

"It was too neatly done, hardly the work of vandals. If I were to guess, I'd say it was an *inside* job, say, someone with a key."

Then, leaning forward so only she could hear his next words, he said, "If I ever catch this *vandal* stealing from me again, this *master* will command her."

He straightened and tossed his credit card onto the counter.

"You pay when you pick them up." Katie lowered her eyes briefly. His last statement had shaken her up so much she had to force herself to glance back up at him. She was determined to hold her own with this man.

He snatched up the card and stalked out of the store.

A few minutes later, Katie entered Phil's Diner and was immediately met with the sound of chinking flatware against pottery and the hum of voices across the restaurant. Over crab cakes and a salad, Katie, irate from her encounter with Max, poured out the whole incident to Jill.

"The arrogance of the man, threatening me like I'm some, some ..."

"Thief?" Jill said in hushed tones. "He knows." Jill's eyes filled with anxiety. "And to think I aided and abetted."

"He has no proof, and if he did, you're not involved. You didn't even come near the house, much less in it."

"You'd better watch out, Katie."

Katie looked across the table at her friend. "Master me, will he? Well, we'll soon see about that." A small smile tugged at the corners of her mouth.

Jill's forehead creased in a frown. "What are you saying?"

"He obviously left the house in quite a hurry this morning, before opening any of the doors." Katie grinned.

Jill's frown deepened.

"The *Master* has another surprise awaiting him." Katie's instincts told her to be terrified, but frankly she couldn't wait for his reaction. "It seems Round Two will go to me as well."

After lunch, Katie was just about to open the door to Rods n' Reels when Max pushed it open from the inside, almost slamming it into her face. She hastily stepped back onto the sidewalk. Startled, she looked up into Max's rugged features, still affected by his good looks.

"Forget something?"

Max glared down at her, his jaw tightening at her question.

"It seems our town thief also stole most of the hinges from the doors as well. I've just finished placing the order for new ones. Amazingly, there's been a run on knobs *and* hinges lately."

Katie shrugged and moved to pass him. Max lifted his arm, blocking her entry. Katie tensed as he leaned toward her.

"Don't let this little victory go to your head because it won't last long, angel. If I were you, I'd start watching your back."

He dropped his arm. Licking dry lips, Katie lifted her chin and pushed her way past his massive form. She sensed his power and strength as she stepped through the doorway, pressing her back against the frame and away from him as she did so. Her hips and chest brushed against his rock hard body causing a physical reaction to shoot through her. Such close proximity caused a strange sensation in her limbs, weakening them as she made her way to the counter.

It took Katie only seconds to look up his order and a few seconds more for her to make the change. He worked fast, but not fast enough. Her fingernails flew across the computer keys in search of his order. "Here's something I'm sure he'll be needing." She chuckled. And the item was only one letter off from what he'd actually ordered, which, when discovered, would easily explain the clerical error.

The next day after church, Katie worked in her studio at her aunt's house and finished another watercolor that evening. The Little River Light sat proudly, yet simply, on a grassy knoll bordered by rocks and a surging sea. With careful selections of color and hue, Katie made sure her paintings would complement each other when hung in the same space. "*If* they were ever hung," she muttered. Sally Batson still hadn't returned her call, and Katie worried if she ever would.

## Chapter 9

"You should have seen the place," Jill exclaimed. "I've never seen so many carpenters, electricians, and plumbers. The last time I saw such activity was at the Junior League's Designer Show House in Baltimore last year. It's obvious he's renovating the main house, but shouldn't he be adding on if he's turning it into a swank hotel?"

"I don't know."

"I told you not to fly over there in a tizzy until you knew for sure."

Katie let out a heavy sigh. "I'm dying to know what he's up to. What I need is real access to the place. You know, like on a daily basis. Then I can find out what he's really up to. I just know it's a hotel. What else could it be?" A sudden idea brightened her mood. Something Pop would call 'mischief making.' "You know something, Jill, I think I kind of like the idea of Pop moving into the light station after all."

That afternoon, as Katie pushed her cart down the canned vegetable aisle in Paige's Market, she ran into Mrs. G.

"Hello, Katie. I heard you moved into your aunt's house." At Katie's look of surprise, she added, "Bessie told me."

"Yes, I'm living there for a while, just long enough to finish the project I'm working on. So how have you been? What's going on with you?"

"I'm doing well, thank you. And right now I'm just

picking up something for dinner. I'm having the son of an old friend over tonight and am anxious to catch up on his family."

"Well, that's great. Anyone I know?"

Mrs. G hesitated only slightly before responding. "Well, actually, I believe you have met him—Max Sawyer."

"Max Sawyer's mother is your old friend?" Katie asked in surprise.

"Yes, we met in college. Beth also has a degree in education. Although she stopped teaching once she had her boys."

An idea began to form in Katie's mind. "So, he'll be coming over for dinner tonight?"

"That's right. I'm so looking forward to it. I haven't had a chance to spend any time with him since he acquired the light station. Apparently, he's been quite busy with that project. Well, I must run, dear. It was so good seeing you."

"Same here, Mrs. G." *And I hope you keep him talking all evening.*


Katie dared not risk Max's possible unexpected return, so she waited a full fifteen minutes after he drove off before she approached the station. The key slipped perfectly into the lock of the keeper's house. Even though she felt confident she would not be interrupted, her heart thudded loudly in her chest. Once inside, she turned on a small flashlight, then gasped out loud. All of her parents' furniture was gone. Frantically, she rushed through the first floor, and except for a variety of carpentry tools, sawhorses, and ladders, the place was empty.

She took the stairs two at a time to check out the second floor. Upstairs, all of the doors were closed, and sheets of plastic were taped over them. She pulled one of the sheets back and pushed the door open. The beam of light landed on a mass of furniture neatly stored and stacked with quilts as padding all throughout the room. She let out a pure sigh of relief. He hadn't gotten rid of it. She secured the tape and plastic back over the door and entered the next room. Here was her parents' dining room set, as well as all of the kitchen pieces and the two, wingback chairs from her dad's study. On impulse, she crossed the room and removed all of the sterling flatware from the sideboard drawers and quickly wrapped them in her jacket. Relief spread over her as she took great pains to secure the plastic over this door as well so *he* wouldn't know anything had been disturbed.

Back downstairs, she walked through each room taking stock of the work already completed. Katie was amazed at how much had been renovated and how quickly. Convinced it had to be shoddy workmanship, Katie pointed the light onto the crown molding, inspecting it under the high beam of the flashlight. It was beautiful. "Money does indeed talk," she said as she snapped off the light.

Katie turned the handle, making sure the front door was securely locked, then quickly walked to the cottage. When she stepped inside, utter longing surged in her breast. Oh, how she missed her little cottage. She gazed around the tiny dwelling and except for a few items that pointed to a definite masculine presence, Max had not changed a thing. She smiled as she noted the handles were still missing and the doors were stacked and leaning against one of the walls. Glancing at her watch, she realized she had been on the property more than an hour. She quickly removed her screwdriver to begin the tedious job of removing the upstairs doorknobs. After she finished, Katie snatched up a tea towel and wrapped the silver in it, then bundled the knobs and flatware in her jacket by tying the sleeves.

Headlights cut across the room, making her heart pound. Too late to go through the front door, she quickly let herself out of one of the back windows and dropped to the ground in a quiet thud. Her breaths came in short gasps as she stooped over and hurried away from the cottage. She ducked behind a mass of knockout rose bushes she had planted more than two years ago right as the headlights panned in her direction.

With bated breath, she watched as Max got out of his Z4 and heard the high-pitched double click of the car when he locked it. She watched him through an opening in the hedge as he walked up the front steps. Suddenly he stopped and looked around. Fearing any minute he would hear the loud pounding of her heart, she began to feel faint and realized she had been holding her breath. Lightheaded, she put her head down between her knees to stop the sudden wave of darkness. Her head snapped back up as she heard the sound of a twig snap and realized that it was the clicking of the door as Max turned the knob and entered the cottage. She waited until the door was firmly shut and she saw the inside light flood the multi-paned windows with warm light.

She darted away like a deer in panic. Her chest heaved and her breath came quickly in short, staccato gasps. When she thought it was safe, she stopped, her trembling body collapsing onto the ground. Unlike the last time, she didn't feel at all elated. She felt terrible, like a thief. A sudden spurt of tears filled her eyes. What was she doing? Was she completely crazy? She made her way to her dinghy and pulled out a heavy, oblong metal-and-pine seaman's box from underneath the middle seat. She lifted the rough-hewn lid and stared at the contents within. They stared back at her with mock disdain. Katie unwrapped the doorknobs from her jacket and put them in with the hinges and faucet handles and placed her mother's silver, still wrapped in the towel, beside them. She brushed a tear from her cheek, closed the lid, and began the laborious process of pushing the box back under the seat.

"Tears? Can it be the town thief is sorry for her sins?"

Katie spun around. Max stood there, towering over

her like an avenging angel. He gently shoved her aside and reached for the box. "Let's see what we have here, shall we?" In seconds, he accessed the contents. "My God, you even took the silver?"

Katie could sense, rather then see, his outrage.

"I can explain," she whispered.

"You're damned right you'll explain, and to the sheriff!"

Katie caught her breath on a sob.

Max seemed to hesitate for brief moment. "Too late." His voice was rough with anger as he hauled her to her feet. "You're wasting your tears on me."

Less than an hour later, Katie found herself perched on a lumpy mattress covered in blue and white ticking in one of the three jail cells in the sheriff's office. She sat stunned, still unable to believe that she was sitting locked up in the town jail. Why did she clam up? Why didn't she just tell him the stuff was hers? *Because you'd feel like a fool, spilling it at this late date. And admit it. You like sparing with him.*

Freddy Pendleton, a tall, gangly former Paige Point High basketball player, was dumfounded at the prospect of locking her up and told her so. "Don't worry, Katie. When Sheriff Collins gets back, he'll know what to do."

Twenty minutes later, Freddy brought her a pizza from Phil's Diner and sat with her in the cell while she ate it. Then he produced a deck of cards and proceeded to play a game of gin rummy with her.

"Thank you, Freddy, but shouldn't you be manning your post out front?"

"Teddy's back from his dinner break," he murmured as he placed a full house down in front of her. Freddy and Teddy were identical twins, and even though they were two years older than her, she'd been a cheerleader and had hung out with them frequently during high school, especially after the games.

The action of someone clearing his throat brought both

heads up. Freddy Pendleton quickly shot to his feet.

"Freddy, you're relieved, son." The kindly gray eyes that looked down at her held both a disapproving and a questioning look in them. "You, too, Katie. Come on out of there," the sheriff ordered as he held the bars open.

"I didn't steal from him, sheriff. I promise."

"Well, he says you did and that he caught you red-handed. Can you explain that, girl?"

"I can only say that I did take what he says, but I wasn't stealing."

Sheriff Collins shook his balding head.

"Let's go."

"But ...?"

"I've been talking to Mr. Sawyer, and after a lengthy discussion, he's decided to drop the charges against you."

Katie's eyes flooded with relief.

"But before you get all excited, there's a condition attached." The father of her old school friend, Jane, glared down at her.

"Condition?" Katie asked with mounting apprehension.

"That's right, young lady. I'm putting you on probation for sixty days. During that time you have to work for him at the light station."

"What?"

"You heard right, and if you were standing before a judge, it would be ninety. But this is not a legal thing. I can't make you do it, but it's either that or he assured me he would press charges again, and this time they would stick."

"That scoundrel."

The sheriff stopped walking and studied her. "I don't know about that, but if you want my advice, you'll cooperate. Otherwise, this could really be hard on Angus. Have you even thought about that?"

Katie sagged in defeat.

"Come on, he's out front waiting for you."

When she got to the front office, Max was nowhere in sight. Momentarily, her spirits lifted. Maybe he'd decided to leave without her. Sheriff Collins opened the front door and Katie followed him outside. "Here she is, Mr. Sawyer." The sheriff gave Katie an encouraging pat on the shoulder, told her to behave herself, and disappeared back inside.

Max had not moved forward at her appearance but stood leaning against a light post with his arms folded across his chest. The harsh light from above made his face seem cold and forbidding. His glacial eyes pinned her to the sidewalk, halting her in her steps.

He pushed his hips away from the post. "You should be thankful the sheriff is a friend of yours. Personally, I think a few more nights in a cell would do you some good. Believe me, he's the only reason you're standing out here on the street right now." He paused waiting for some sort of reply, but when none came, he prompted, "Well, have you nothing to say?"

She bit down on her soft lower lip. Earlier, she had wanted so desperately to explain, but now she didn't have the strength or the courage. She just wanted to go home. Katie found herself tensing as Max slowly stepped toward her, took hold of her elbow, and walked her to his car. He stopped in front of the passenger door and without saying a word, opened it for her and gestured for her to get in.

"Where are we going?"

"I'm taking you home." Max spoke with a grim determination.

"I'd rather walk."

The look he gave her told her it would be foolish to argue with him. Katie slid down into the leather seat and couldn't help but notice that for a sports car, the Z4 was extremely comfortable and the red-lit dashboard looked more like the cockpit of an airplane than a car. Within seconds of leaving the curb, she could feel the warmth emanating from the seat soothing her shivering limbs. The nights had now gotten cold, and having left her jacket in her boat, the heat warmed her like a welcoming blanket.

With her hands locked in a death grip, she tried her best to relax and to keep her eyes occupied on the road in front of her. She wondered about her Jeep, but decided not to mention it. She would just walk over and get it in the morning.

About to say something when he passed her aunt's house, she thought better of that as well. As the long, brooding silence ensued, her goal was to get out of his car and behind the closest locked door unscathed. The thought of having to work for this man was unbearable. This evening had certainly not gone as she'd planned.

"I take it you've agreed to my terms," Max said.

"I haven't decided, yet."

"Well, you have about five minutes to make a decision."

"And if I refuse?"

"If you refuse, I will have you arrested for stealing. And the heartbreak Angus suffers over that will be on your head."

"And just what will I do all day, if it's not too much to ask?"

"You'll work for me at the light station. Angus has agreed to help me with my project. Since you'll be at the station for the next sixty days, it would be a lot easier on Angus if you both just moved in for the time being."

"You make it sound like I'm in your custody."

"Believe me, if I could have arranged that, I would have. You ought to be in someone's custody. Look up the word sometime. You might learn something."

Max finally pulled up at the back of Rods n' Reels. Neither said a word as Katie opened the door and scrambled out of the car.

"You have two days to pack your personal belongings and move into the keeper's house. I don't care what story you tell Angus, but I will be expecting him to move in as well."

Tempted to tell him off, she slammed the door instead, ran up the back stairs to her apartment, then stood there until she heard the Z4 pull away. Slowly, she made her way back down the wooden steps and began the short walk to her aunt's house.

She greeted a hungry Buddy, let him in the house, and in seconds set a dish before him. "Sorry, boy." She scratched him through his thick main of golden red fur. "Come on, you can sleep with me tonight. I don't want to be alone."

Dressed in a thick, chocolate-brown sweatshirt and faded blue jeans, Katie walked briskly against the chilly morning air down Main Street toward Rods n' Reels and her apartment. After a fitful night, what she needed was a strong cup of coffee. She trudged her way through town in her warm Uggs with Buddy leashed at her side.

Max stood facing her on the sidewalk. He was frowning, much like he had the night before. Katie stopped abruptly as soon as she noticed him. He was dressed in well-fitted jeans, a wool fisherman's sweater, and dark boots. His thick, dark blond hair was accentuated by the deep blue scarf he'd tied around his neck. His usual air of authority oozed from him. To her annoyance, Buddy greeted him with unabashed delight.

"We need to talk," he said, gesturing her toward the diner.

"I have two days before I have to suffer your company," she stated emphatically as she took a step to go around him.

"Come on, you look like you could use some coffee." He took hold of her arm.

"I don't want any coffee."

"Let me rephrase it then. You and I are going to have a

little talk. The coffee is optional. The talk is not."

Katie jerked her arm out of his grasp, but continued to walk beside him. Outside of Phil's Diner, she looped Buddy's leash around the post provided for that purpose, filled the complimentary canine water bowl, and was forced to precede Max into the warm restaurant as he held the door for her, a challenging glint in his eye.

Phil, Peggy, and several of Katie's former co-workers yelled out a welcome from behind the busy counter and open grill area where breakfast orders were being hollered out. Phil even came over to give Katie a big bear hug and to ask her how she was doing, reminding her that if need be, she always had a job at Phil's. Katie smiled up at him, then introduced him to Max before Phil hurried back to the kitchen.

Max and Katie settled themselves in a booth along the back wall of the diner and ordered coffee.

"Everyone's little darling, aren't you?"

"Can I help it if people like me?"

Max leaned back into the corner of the booth and laid one muscular arm over the back of the bench seat. "Why did you do it? You don't seem the type to steal from people. They would obviously be shocked if they knew." He nodded his head toward the busy open kitchen. "As well as someone else I used to know," he muttered softly.

Katie's gaze flew up to meet his. She wondered who the 'someone else' was as Peggy walked up with the coffee and poured the steaming hot liquid in the two cups before them.

"Cream and sugar?" she asked.

"No, thanks." Max shook his head.

"Just cream for me, Peg."

A moment later, Peggy returned with the cream. "Nothing else, no breakfast for you two?" They both shook their heads.

Katie made a long, deliberate action out of pouring the

cream into her coffee and stirring even slower before she finally glanced up at him. Max had leaned forward having already taken a sip of the black liquid, his lean hands wrapped around his cup like a caress. With his elbows on the table, Max lifted his cup to his lips, then held it there while he took a long, scrutinizing look at her. His deep-set eyes assessed her like she was some sort of specimen.

She lowered her gaze from his and hastily picked up her coffee. In doing so, she sloshed some of the hot liquid on her left hand. White-hot pain shot through her injured flesh and she dropped the cup, which clattered onto the table. She sucked in her breath and grabbed her scalded hand.

"Here, let me look at that."

"It's all right."

"Let me take a look." Max lifted her wrist, then raised his hand, motioning for Peggy, who having seen the accident was already on her way over with ice. Max placed the cold compress gently on her hand and held it there.

She let out a long sigh as the cool surface soothed her throbbing skin. "Really, it's all right," she insisted as she tried to pull her hand away, suddenly self-conscious and very aware of the warmth emanating from his fingers.

Silence filled the space between them while he held the bag of ice in place. After a moment, Max removed the compress to inspect the damage. He gently pressed her icy palm with his thumb, careful of the blister forming on her flesh.

"I think you'll be okay," he said. "If the coffee had been any hotter, we'd be making a doctor's run. Unless you still want to go?"

She shook her head. The pain was easing, but she knew it would be difficult holding a paintbrush for the next day or two. Besides, having Max accompany her to the doctor might be more than she could stand at the moment.

He released her hand and took a sip of coffee from a

freshly poured cup. "So let's have it."

"Let's have what?"

"Don't be obtuse. I'm not in the mood. Why in blazes would you steal from me? Is that what you were doing that first night I found you in the cottage?"

"No!"

"You have something against me, and I'd like to know what it is."

Katie looked grudgingly down at her cup, at the caramel liquid staring back at her. It was still too painful. He didn't know she was the other bidder, so how could she tell him that the thought of his winning bid was unbearable for her. That every day she saw herself in that town hall meeting, in shock as she watched her future home slip away, unable to do anything about it. That she relived that moment over and over, and that every time she looked at him, she realized again her acute loss. How could she tell him how much it angered her that one with money and power could attain what she for lack of money could not? Not to mention how much it galled her to stand by and watch him redo all of her hard work. Wasn't it enough that she loved it? Had worked hard for it? Didn't that count for something? He didn't love the lighthouse, but because he wanted it, he got it. Oh, she wanted to tell him all right, to hurl the truth of it into his smug face.

Instead she found herself saying, "At this point it really doesn't matter."

"Forgive me if I disagree. You're belligerent, and you have a chip on your shoulder the size of Manhattan whenever you're around me. Would it be too much to ask to at least strive for some peace between us? For Angus's sake if nothing else? He'll think it's pretty odd if we're at each other's throats all the time."

Katie looked up at that with a scowl.

"I can see we're getting nowhere with this conversation."

He all but slammed his cup in the saucer. "I'll be gone for the next couple of days, and I'll expect you to be moved in along with Angus when I get back. For the time being, you can take the suite of rooms upstairs in the keeper's house."

"Fine," she said in a clipped tone.

Max's eyes narrowed at her quick reply. "Not thinking of skipping out, are you?" His eyes held a mocking light she was getting used to seeing.

"No, I wouldn't do that to Pop. You made it quite clear what the ramifications would be if I didn't comply with you.

"Good, I'm glad to see we're on the same wavelength for a change. Although I hardly expect it will last," he drawled sarcastically. "Come on, I'll see you home."

"You don't need to do that."

"Well, I'm going to anyway."

"I have to get my Jeep."

"It's already been taken care of."

Buddy, with tail wagging, greeted them both when they came out of the front entrance, blissfully unaware of the animosity between them as they walked in silence to the hardware store.

# Chapter 10

If Pop was surprised about her announcement to move into the keeper's house, he certainly didn't show it. It was as if he'd been expecting it.

"Yes, Max told me he'd finally convinced you to move in. I know I don't have to tell you how pleased I am about it. You were right all along, Katie, it's what I've wanted ever since I had to move out years ago when the Coast Guard automated the light."

Somewhat bemused, Katie wondered how it was that Max seemed to know such intimate details about Pop as she unloaded the last of her things into the smaller of the two bedrooms in the suite. It was beautifully restored using celery green and white with pale blue accents. She was pleased to see the entire suite decorated with her mom and dad's furniture.

Pop's room was in browns and creamy hues with a smattering of details in black and red. Really beautiful. It was obvious Max had used a design firm, for it certainly had that professional touch. Katie's heart surged in jealousy, wishing she'd had the chance to decorate it. What was it Max had said about the décor of the cottage when she'd first met him? 'Just a little too feminine for my tastes.' Well, fine. He could paint it purple for all she cared.

Katie arranged for Bessie to help Pop move the rest of his things in, as she would be going to the island for the next two days.

One hour later, dressed in jeans, a leaf green cap, and matching cabled T-neck ribbed sweater, Katie pulled in to her usual spot on the beach. She tossed her backpack ashore and hopped onto the sand with both feet, thankful she'd beat the storm that was moving in.

She slung the pack onto her shoulder and made her way to the cabin. She stopped short upon entering the small clearing where the cabin sat, surprised to see smoke coming from the chimney. Katie hesitated, then decided to circle around through the thicket of brush to approach the cabin from the rear. Coming up along side the log structure, she craned her neck to peek in through the window and to her consternation saw none other than Max Sawyer laying logs to the fire. Eyes widening, she watched him stand up and head for the front door. She ducked back down and at the sound of the squeaky door hinges and quickly ran back toward the beach. Then she saw it—his cruiser—docked a few feet offshore. A Sea Ray 58 Sedan Bridge, she thought in open admiration. Davy would have loved owning a fishing boat like that. On impulse, Katie jumped in the rubber raft that was perched onto the sand and paddled the short distance to the boat, climbed over the back, and jumped on board. Crouching, she moved along the outside of the cabin, then entered quickly, her eyes scanning the control panel until finally locating the key. *Pay dirt!* Gleeful, she snatched it off the dashboard, then tossed it over the side. That would serve him right for not only stealing her lighthouse but her own private getaway island as well. She quickly scurried off the back of the boat and into the raft, still bobbing on the shallow water. After returning to the beach, she secured the raft, then hurried across the tip of the island to where her dinghy was moored.

Both hands on the bow, she shoved off with both feet hitting the floorboards at the same time. She reached for the starter key, but it wasn't there. Frantically, she scanned the bottom of the boat.

"Looking for this?" Max stood on the shore, legs

slightly apart, wearing cargo pants and a dark sweater. In his right hand, he held up the key.

Katie spun around so fast she almost toppled over. *No way.* At that point, she was about ten feet off shore and frantically reached for the oars.

"They're not there, either," came the sharp tone of Max's deep voice.

Katie sat down abruptly. Her legs had all but turned to jelly.

"Yes, that's right." He smiled across the water at her. "You are well and truly stranded."

Katie tugged off her shoes, hopped over the side, and pulled the dinghy through the water, heaving it onto the sand. She quickly slipped back into her shoes, took a deep breath, then turned, ready for the confrontation she knew was coming. But Max was already striding away from her. Katie stared at his departing back and groaned inwardly. There was nothing else to do but follow. She walked behind him back across the island tip and realized he was making for his cruiser. Knowing what he would find or more like what he wouldn't find, she hurried toward the cabin. Yanking open the door, Katie threw herself inside, then turned quickly to slam the bolt across the doorframe. "What the ...?" Katie's hand stilled over the place where the bolt had been.

Max threw the cabin door open, then waited, half-expecting to be hit with a frying pan or something equally as painful.

"Where's my deadbolt?" Katie scowled up at him.

"It seems you're not the only one who can remove hardware." He stood in the doorway, blocking any attempt on her part to leave. She was adorable standing there, all blue-eyed and battle-ready, like a startled kitten, back arched and hissing.

Katie clamped her eyes shut and shook her head. "What are you doing here? How do you even know about this place?"

"A little bird told me."

"Pop." Katie stomped her foot. "Is nothing sacred?"

"Apparently not. Now, where's my key?" He held out his hand.

Her gaze flew upward and to the left. "I—I don't have your key."

Just what he feared. At least he had a duplicate back at the keeper's house. "Well, in that case, I guess you and I will just be stuck here for a while."

He watched Katie's eyes widen in panic as she pushed her way past him, then sprinted back to where his boat was docked. He pulled the cabin door closed behind him and took his time following her. Yes, he was certainly going to enjoy this.

He caught her picking up a wide, flat piece of bark, no doubt intending on using it as an oar.

"If what I suspect is correct, that you've disposed of my boat key, I suggest you go into the water and look for it, while you still have daylight left."

Her mouth gaped open. "Are you crazy? That could take forever."

"Then you'd better get started, hadn't you, angel?" He stifled a grin at her startled, wide-eyed discomfort and watched, with pure enjoyment, the gamut of emotions that played across her flushed cheeks. This kitten was trapped, and she knew it.

Katie raised her fisted hand to her mouth. "Why can't we take my boat since you obviously have the key to it?"

"Because there's a storm coming, in case you hadn't noticed, and we wouldn't make it. And that, frankly, is why I have your key. Added to the fact that I knew as soon as you found out I was here, you'd hightail it out of here, getting yourself in all kinds of trouble. Then I'd have to risk my yacht, not to mention my neck, to go after you. And now you've thrown out my key?"

"Okay, geez, I'll go get it." Katie bent down and pulled off her shoes and socks.

*Unbelievable. She's actually going in the water.*

He watched as Katie rolled up her jeans as high as they would go, then stepped gingerly into the chilly October water, stopping when it hit her knees.

A disgruntled expression appeared on her face. He loved the way her forehead creased when she was put out about something. The way her gorgeous eyes clouded over. He watched as she placed her small hands on either side of her head, pushing her hair away from her face. He gazed at her exquisite profile as she looked down at the water. He shook his head. Only God knew how he longed to cup her face in his hands. Run his fingers through her honey gold hair.

It had completely floored him when he'd caught her stealing. Here he thought he was returning to his sweet little lighthouse girl, only to be met with an annoying juvenile delinquent and the most maddening creature this side of the Atlantic. Damned if he wasn't confused. He was sure of one thing though: she needed reining in, guidance, and a firm hand. And he'd be the one to do it.

Reaching into his jacket, he pulled a cheroot from the inside pocket. He tilted his head forward as he struck a match to the small cigar, signaling to Katie that he was in no hurry. Exhaling, he watched her through the rising smoke.

"I can't find it. I'm sorry." Huge pleading eyes turned toward him.

He was almost undone by that darling look of appeal. But instead he took a steadying breath. *Stay focused, man.* Then sat down in one easy motion onto the ground. "Keep looking, angel."

Ten minutes later, shivering, she pleaded, "It's getting dark."

"Then I suggest you get on your knees and feel around for it."

"My feet are numb."

Max got up and put his hand in the water. "Not that cold." He tossed the cigar butt into the water.

"You're littering," she snapped.

*She's got spunk, that's for sure.* "It's biodegradable." He pointed back toward the water before settling himself down on the beach.

Gritting her teeth together, Katie pushed up her sleeves before reaching down to continue her search. "You're enjoying this, aren't you?"

"Immensely."

"Tell me, was it your military training or have you always had this *charming* personality?" After a few minutes, she said, "This is impossible, and you know it. I'm done."

Black thunderclouds loomed like a giant over the island, bringing with them huge gusts of wind. Without warning, a surge of water hit Katie full force and knocked her over. Heartbeat spiking, Max stood and headed for the water as she squealed and struggled to get up, only to be hit again. Splanttering and coughing, she tried to stand, but was immediately knocked down yet again.

Reaching into the cooler than expected water, Max grasped Katie's arms and pulled her drenched, pathetic form out of the water. She slid down onto the gritty beach and with trembling hands wiped her hair out of her face.

"Had enough?" he said, feeling a wave of self-recrimination wash through him. He'd taken the joke too far.

"I lo—loathe you," she whispered through chattering teeth.

"I'm sure you do, angel."

"I'm n-not your a-angel." Katie huddled on the sand

before him, shivering, and hugging her arms around her torso.

He felt like a heel. No, worse than a heel. He rubbed his hand around the back of his neck, swore, snatched up her shoes, then bent down and scooped her up in his arms. He reveled in the feel of her trembling body as she burrowed into the warmth of his chest. As he tightened his arms around her, a raw ache filled him. An ache coupled with the longing for this charade to be over. When he reached the cabin, he kicked the door open with one booted foot, then lowered her onto a chair in front of the fire.

"Get those wet things off," he commanded as he strode across the room, returning in seconds with several towels and a warm blanket. He stood, hovering over her as she struggled to remove her turtleneck. With a sigh, he reached forward, grabbed hold of the wet mass that was now gathered around her shoulders and yanked everything up and over her head ignoring her heated protests in the process. Katie threw her arms across her lacy bra. Her cheeks flushed adorably in embarrassment. He wrapped a blanket around her, then bent down and began to unsnap her jeans.

"No!" Katie threw one hand against his chest while the other clutched the blanket.

"Yes," he answered calmly, but stopped at the frantic look in her eyes.

Another wave of recrimination shot through him. What had come over him? Bullying a helpless young woman. He'd clearly terrified her.

Feeling a muscle clench and unclench in his jaw, he said, "I'll leave you to get undressed on your own."

When he returned, Katie had the blanket clutched around her. He handed her a towel and as she wordlessly dried her hair, he caught a whiff of seaweed and salt water mingled with fresh squeezed lemons. Standing so close to her, knowing she was naked beneath the blanket, Max struggled against taking her in his arms right then and there and telling her he was her sailor and the last person to see her brother alive. He wanted to confront her with her aunt's accusations to see if she felt the same. He glanced at her, and caught her staring. Her cheeks flushed crimson as she quickly lowered her eyes. He'd made her uncomfortable, again.

"Hang your clothes in front of the fire. I'm going to change."

By the time he returned, Katie had gotten most of the dampness out of her hair and was already curled up in the upholstered chair looking like a gift to be unwrapped. She flushed scarlet when he deliberately took note of her bra and panties hanging near the fire. His lips quirked, which had her tugging the blanket snugly around her. He stepped toward her and watched her eyes widen. As he neared her, he knew her heart was beating like a drum, if the rise and fall of her chest was any indication. He reached over her, brushing the top of her head with his chest and picked up the brandy on the table behind her. Wordlessly, he filled two small glasses.

"Drink this. It'll help." He watched as something close to relief spread across her face.

Katie raised the amber liquid to her lips and grimaced. "Where did you get this?"

Max lowered his frame into the other chair, stretched out his legs, and eyed her over the rim of his glass. "It came off the *Sting Ray*. The refrigerator is also well stocked so dinner will be ready shortly.

"While you do that, I'll go and change."

"Good idea. Get something warm on while I fix us something to eat."

When Katie returned about ten minutes later, Max was surprised to see her wearing flannel PJs and an oversized sweatshirt. Taking in the feminine rosebud pattern of her PJs, he couldn't stop the slight quirking of his lips as he set two plates filled with eggs, sausage, and toast on the low table in front of them.

"Off to bed, are you?"

"It's the warmest thing I have here."

They sat down and polished off the simple meal in minutes.

Over coffee, Katie said in a small voice, "I'm sorry I took your keys."

Max studied her, taking in the hollow in her cheeks, the blue tinge around her mouth. He set down his cup, then took her hand in his, running a thumb along the smooth surface of her skin. "And I'm sorry for being a pig-headed lout. I should have been paying more attention to the weather. Are you sure you're okay?"

She gave a soft smile. "I'm fine. It—It's my fault, too. I knew I was getting cold, but I didn't want you to win. I wanted you to feel bad for..." Her gaze grew faraway.

Dammit. What was he missing? "For what, angel?"

She shook her head. "Nothing." She cleared her throat. "So how come you're here? I thought you were going away for a couple of days."

He gave an inward sigh. He'd get to the bottom of her hatred of him, but would play along, for the moment. "I went back by the house to pick up something and Angus told me about the upcoming storm and where you'd gone. He was worried because you wouldn't answer your phone. So here I am, angel, to the rescue." He grinned at her.

"I didn't need rescuing as I'm sure you well know."

"From where I'm sitting, that's debatable."

"You want to be a nuisance," she said.

"And you stole all the hardware from me."

"I did not ..." Katie clamped her mouth shut, then met his gaze straight on. "Things are not always what they seem, Mr. Sawyer."

"No truer words have ever been said." He raised his

glass to her in salute. He knew what he was hiding from her. But what was she keeping from him?

Katie periodically glanced at Max from behind a magazine, while he sat making notes in his cell phone. She had to admit, his profile, that square jaw and those firm lips, slightly parted, just a few feet from her, created quite the male specimen. She sat riveted by the frowning intensity in his eyes. Her heart jumped an octave when he turned and looked at her.

"I'm going to bed now." She stood abruptly as she spoke.

"Be my guest. You don't see me stopping you." Max settled himself more comfortably in his chair.

Open-mouthed, Katie snapped, "I suggest you go settle yourself on your yacht."

"Go out in this mess, not on your life, angel." The wind had picked up, and it had started raining hard.

"Well you certainly can't sleep here."

"I don't see a problem. I'll take the top bunk, and you can have the bottom."

About to argue, Katie glanced upward, remembering that the top mattress was moldy from recent rains and decided to let him find out the hard way.

"Fine," she replied and pulled a paperback novel out of her backpack before crawling between the sheets of the bottom bunk. When she realized she'd read the same paragraph for the fourth time, she gave herself a mental shake and started the chapter over. An entire chapter later, she still couldn't tell what she had read if her life depended on it. It was quite disconcerting having Max sprawled out in a chair less than ten feet away from her. Giving up, she snapped the book shut, turned on her side, and closed her eyes. It was all Katie could do to relax. She couldn't help it. She opened her eyes and caught Max staring at her with a satirical look that sent her pulse racing. Exasperated, she turned over and punched her pillow under her head, this time placing her back to him.

Exhaustion seemed to creep into her limbs as sleep began to overtake her. Soon, all she was aware of was the occasional crackling of the fire and the turning of a page in his book.

An hour later, after Katie was finally asleep, Max cursed as he took note of the moldy mattress encased in the top bunk. Hopping down, his thick wool socks muffling any sound his tall frame might otherwise have made, he grabbed his pillow, then looked around the cabin as if he didn't already know what his only option was. After a brief hesitation, he slid onto the narrow bunk next to Katie's still form. She moaned and turned toward him in an action that enabled him to slip his left arm underneath her head and neck. He held his breath, awaiting the inevitable firestorm that would ensue when she awakened. Instead, she curled against him and nested her head against his chest. Dear God, he was in heaven. With bated breath, he watched as she burrowed her supple form next to his as if it was the most natural thing in the world. Thoughts not in the least peculiar washed over him, but he held himself in check for another time and another place. His lips quirked as it occurred to him how pleasant she was when she was sleeping; that impulsive, aggravating mouth of hers finally quiet. He held perfectly still until he fell asleep listening to her gentle even breathing.

Katie's eyes fluttered open. The howling of the wind had grown stronger, causing the shutters to bang against the window. She squeezed her eyes against the battering and realized something hard was lying across her waist. She drew her hand up to her waist to push it off before her eyes flew open in horror. Max's arm was clasped over her midriff against her bare flesh. She jumped up, hitting her head on the underside of the top bunk as she did so.

"Ow!"

Max woke with a start, sending the sheet and blanket flying every which way. Katie held her aching head as she scurried out at the foot of the bed. She landed on the floor in a massive heap, the blanket following close behind.

Max groaned. "What the devil?"

"Get out of my bed," she managed to squeak out.

Max raised himself up on one elbow and eyed her across the foot of the bed. "The top bunk was a mess."

"I am not sleeping in the same bed as you."

"Suit yourself, but the blanket stays with me." Max lunged forward, snatching the blanket from the floor.

Shivering, Katie hurried over to the fire to add logs to the smoldering embers. She dragged one of the upholstered chairs as close to the flames as she deemed safe and curled up in a tight little ball, trying in vain to get warm. She slept fitfully for about fifteen minutes just to awaken again as the cold penetrated her limbs. Putting the last of the logs on the fire, she curled up once more in the chair, succumbing to sleep as she felt the beginnings of warmth just to awaken shivering minutes later. Totally exhausted, Katie huddled in the chair, her knees drawn up to her chest and her jaw clamped tightly together in an attempt to keep her teeth from chattering. She looked longingly over at the warm bed. Max had his back to her, and she could tell he wasn't shivering.

Miserably cold, she could stand it no longer. She sprung from the confines of the chair, lifted the covers of the blanket and climbed in beside Max's warm body. Lifting his head, he turned and looked over his shoulder as she planted herself against his warm body.

"Don't say a word." Teeth chattering, she practically

burrowed into his broad back.

Max turned over and pulled her in his arms. Nervous tension wracked her body as her heart hammered against her ribs.

"Relax, angel, I'm too tired."

With his arm flung over her midriff, she felt trapped. "I—I need to get back behind you." She spoke in a whisper, unable to look at him.

A peculiar light shone in his tawny eyes. Compressing his lips together, he rolled away from her, shaking his head. With her arms bent at the elbows and her fists gathered beneath her chin, she pressed her shivering limbs against his broad back. She lifted her head slightly as Max reached back to pull her arm over his waist, forcing her to relax against him.

"Go to sleep, Katie," Max murmured into the pillow.

His body warmth slowly invaded her limbs and she couldn't help but relax against him. She drew her legs up, tucking herself against him. Locked and secure, like pieces of a puzzle, they fell asleep.

Katie stirred against the massive enveloping warmth, sighed, and snuggled even closer. "Buddy," she whispered, her eyes still closed.

"Well, that's a first," Max said in a husky whisper, followed by a low chuckle above her head.

*What? Who?* Katie jerked wide-awake, stiffening in Max's arms.

"What's a first?" She forced herself to breathe slowly to combat the panic surging through her.

"Being compared to a dog by the woman in my bed," came the sarcastic reply. "But since I know how much you love Buddy, I guess I can take that as a compliment."

Katie scowled and pushed against his chest.

"I'm just getting up." Max climbed out of the narrow bed, pulling the covers back over her as he did so. "You can stay there until I get breakfast going if you like," he stated with a cheeriness that had her immediately suspicious and wondering what had happened during the night. For the life of her, she couldn't remember anything that would have caused his sunny disposition.

Since it was freezing in the cabin, Katie opted to obey for a change and snuggled into the pillow, more from embarrassment than anything else. She must have fallen back to sleep because when next she opened her eyes, it was to the smell of coffee and sausage. She raised her head and looked sleepily around the room until her eyes came to rest on khaki-clad lean hips and broad shoulders standing over the stove deftly turning sausage, retrieving hot toast and sipping coffee as he did so. As if sensing her perusal, Max turned and cast those seemingly all-knowing brown eyes in her direction.

"It's about time. The fire is almost out, and I'm not putting any more logs on it. We leave in twenty minutes, and if you want breakfast, it's right now."

Why did he always try to boss her around? Katie gritted her teeth. "If it's all the same to you, I'm staying another day, so if you'll just leave me my key ..."

"No way, angel. This weather's going to get a lot worse, and since there's a break in it right now, I want to leave as soon as possible."

*Insufferable!* She willed herself to climb out from under the warm covering. He could have at least kept the fire going. Once her bare feet hit the cold wood planks, she rushed into the bathroom, then stripped off her flannels for a quick sponge bath. When she finally sat down at the table, Max had all but polished off his plate. She ate quickly, then cleaned the dishes and made the bed while Max turned off the generator and stacked wood in the fireplace, making it ready for the next visit.

They walked out to Max's boat, checking for any storm damage along the way. When they arrived, Katie noticed that her dinghy was already tied to the back of his Sea Ray and the rubber raft was on the shore ready for their departure.

Once onboard, Katie settled herself on the leather passenger seat near the steering wheel. The engine purred to life and the Sea Ray sped across the few short miles to the lighthouse pier in Paige Point. Neither spoke during the short journey, so Katie took these few minutes to look at her tormentor. Her eyes roamed from his well-fitting khakis to his thick navy cabled sweater. She gazed at his strong hands that steadied the wheel, reminding her of their gentle strength as he'd drawn her to the warmth of his body the night before. A thought that brought a wave of heat to her cheeks. She took particular note of how his dark blond hair fell in thick waves from his high forehead to the collar of his jacket. His face still held a hint of the bronze warmth of the autumn sun, which displayed his strong chin, straight nose, and tawny, deep-set eyes to perfection. She grudgingly admitted it was still the most strikingly handsome face she had ever seen. Although, he seemed hard and unyielding, she knew in her heart, he could be depended on in a crisis, could be trusted with one's deepest secrets. Startled at such a thought, a peculiar longing stirred within her. She instinctively knew she was part of the problem, but she couldn't help always wanting go against him. There was something about him that called her to battle stations whenever she was around him. Suddenly, she developed an acute yearning for him to like her, to trust her, to be for her and not against her, to have a special place in his life, instead of having her arrested.

"I can't believe you had me locked up," she blurted out.

"That's because you're a thief," he calmly replied as he slowed the Sea Ray and maneuvered it alongside the dock. "And I hardly call your experience in the slammer one of suffering. I heard that deputy brought you pizza, then sat in the cell with you playing cards all evening."

"I went to high school with him and his brother."

"Figures."

"You still had me locked up," she couldn't help but repeat. She tugged at the hem of her jacket in frustration, not ready to explain herself to someone like him. "So who brought you the extra key this morning?"

"No one."

Katie eyed him suspiciously. "What do you mean no one?"

Max grinned at her as he pulled back on the throttle, cutting off the engine. "Just that, angel. I always keep a spare key onboard."

The full realization of his words slammed into her. "Why you despicable, lying ... reprobate! You ... you hateful, despicable ..."

"You already used that word," he stated blandly as he stepped away from the wheel to tie the rope onto the post.

Irate, Katie stood up to follow him. "Despicable, despicable," she ranted back at him. "You deliberately kept me on that island when you knew I didn't want to be there with you. It's bad enough I have to spend two months with you ... and that you've manipulated Pop as well in this blatant charade of yours ... and ..."

"Can you swim?" Max turned abruptly, breaking into her tirade.

"What?" Katie blinked sharply at him, not at all pleased with the interruption.

"Can you swim?"

"What kind of idiot question is that? Of course I can swim."

A sudden trepidation came over her at the determined light that appeared in his eyes. She turned to run, but Max grabbed her by the waist and picked her up.

"No. Don't." Katie flung her arms around his neck. Hanging on for dear life, her heart thudded madly in her chest. As she felt his arms tighten their hold around her, relief spread through her like a wildfire ripping through dry grass. She clung to him until her heart rate slowed to a lighthearted skip. She reveled in the strength of his arms and chest. It was nothing like Davy's crushing big brother hugs or Pop's frail embrace. Katie unclasped her arms from around his neck, lifted her head, and looked up at him. A sudden longing tugged someplace deep within her, making her weak all over. Max lowered his head. His deep brown eyes locked with hers in a spell, rich with promise. She lifted her face—his mouth close to hers—and held her breath. Suddenly she found herself falling through the air. She shrieked as her backside hit the cushioned seat immediately below her. She watched, open-mouthed, as Max's long strides put as much distance between them as possible. Chagrined, she climbed out of the boat and onto the pier, then stalked up to the house.

"Katie, darlin', what happened? You look like a hen that's been thrown off her nest," Pop said.

Teeth clenching, she glared at Max, who sat comfortably by the fire, a humorous light in his eyes. She hated that he knew she'd wanted him to kiss her.

Pop looked back and forth between them, bushy white eyebrows raised with a 'would someone please explain' expression.

"She does look a bit ruffled," Max said with a slow, crooked grin.

"How about a nice cup of tea?" Pop asked, a knowing gleam in his wise eyes.

"Jail would have been preferable to this," Katie muttered as she entered the kitchen.

## Chapter 11

The next morning, Katie followed Max up the mellowed pine stairs to a small bedroom that had been converted to a study. An acute pang hit her upon entering the space as it was tastefully decorated with her father's antique table desk. Max sat her down across from it and calmly took the leather swivel chair opposite. He proceeded to mete out the *house rules* as he termed them with an obvious gloating fervor. She was to keep all of the structures on the property clean as well as cook all of their meals, neither of which worried her. She was no stranger to hard work.

"Of course, you may keep working for Tom and Lily on Saturdays," Max continued.

"I'm sure they'll appreciate it," she said, her voice dripping with sarcasm.

"I'd also like for you to ask permission before you leave the property."

Katie laughed. "You're joking, right?"

"No. There'll be two crews, working two separate shifts. Carpenters, plumbers, electricians, and painters will be all over this property. The pace will be extremely hectic. You simply cannot just leave at the slightest whim. Think you can handle it?"

"I can handle it. It just sounds a lot like *prison* to me." He had a lot of gall trying to order her around.

"It does, doesn't it?" Max stood, signifying that the meeting was over.

Katie squared her shoulders and followed him down the stairs.

"I have to leave for a couple of days," he said as he wrote down his cell number and handed it to her. "I've already gone over everything with my foreman, but call me if you have any questions. Now, I believe there is some hardware that needs your attention."

The next two days flew by for Katie. The work Max had given her was both demanding and physical. Although she weathered it well, she found that she still fell into bed each night quite exhausted.

Jill was Katie's only confidant during that time.

"You have to tell him. Just go up to him and say, 'I want my things back.' This whole thing has gotten out of hand. It—it's ridiculous."

"If I tell him now, I'll not only look like a fool, but I'll miss the chance to find out what he's planning for the station." Katie shifted her cell phone to her other ear and continued. "Why do you think I agreed to this charade to begin with? Now I'll have the run of the place and can look in any drawer that I want. In the meantime, I've got to figure out a way to finish those watercolors and make that deadline."

Max returned two days later, right on schedule. Katie led him through the house, showing him the work she'd finished in his absence.

"As you can see, all hinges and handles accounted for. Would you like me to cancel the replacement orders?"

"No, I'm going to use those in the keeper's house."

She nodded, fully aware of the surprise his order would bring. Following him into the parlor, she was surprised to see Max plop down in the club chair and close his eyes.

"Um, are you okay?"

He opened his eyes and stared at her. "Sympathy? Now that's an unexpected change."

Katie clamped her lips together, then turned and left the room. In minutes, she was back with a hot cup of coffee. "Here, drink this."

Max took the cup and sipped it before placing it on the coffee table. "Thanks. I'm just beat. Too many irons in the fire."

She couldn't help but stare at him. She was witnessing a side of Max that she hadn't seen. Vulnerable and kind of sweet. For just an instant, he reminded her of Jamey.

"How would you like to decorate the rest of this place?" he asked.

"What?"

"And I don't mean just picking out paint and wallpaper. I mean managing the project. Making decisions, placing orders, dealing with the contractors."

"What happened to the person who did the upstairs?"

"Morning sickness. Apparently, she suffers from it all day."

"Oh. Well, sure if you want me to."

It was all she could do to contain her excitement. Her imagination ran wild. She, Katie McCullough, would actually get to decorate the keeper's house, and with someone else's money.

The Friday before Thanksgiving, Katie dressed in her uniform as she called it, khaki pants, a white long-sleeve sweater, and docksides, then skipped down the stairs to the familiar sound of saws and hammering. She slipped on her jacket and stepped outside to say good-morning and was met by someone she hadn't seen before. He approached her with a smile and a handshake.

"Hi, I'm Nate," he quickly informed her, "Max's brother."

Katie opened her mouth in surprise. "Oh, hello." Then

giving his hand a firm shake, she said, "I'm sorry, I'm Katie. Would you like some coffee?" At his nod, Katie invited him inside the cottage. "We'll have to go in here. They're working on the first floor of the keeper's house."

"No problem, that's actually why I'm here. I was on my way to Washington, D.C., and Max wanted me to come by and do a walk-through. He's thinking about adding on to the main house and wanted my opinion."

Katie's fingers stilled on the coffee pot, then she continued to pour the hot liquid. "Cream and sugar?"

"Black is fine." He smiled at her as she handed him the mug.

"So he's thinking of adding on," she said, keeping her voice steady as she refilled her mug.

"He is. I'm a structural engineer, and he wants me to make sure the original structure is sound. I've seen him take less than this and turn it into a prime piece of real estate. This is good," he added as he sipped on the Starbucks Verona blend. "So you're Katie. We've heard a lot about you and Angus."

"Nate, you scoundrel, why didn't you let me know you were coming today?" Max had entered by the back door, and the brothers embraced like two football players in the end zone after a touchdown. Slapping each other's backs, they stood apart, both bursting forth with speech at the same time. Max asked about their folks and their two younger brothers, and Nate responded.

"You're cutting this trip awfully close. Don't tell me you won't be home for Thanksgiving again this year."

"No chance. I'm only spending a few days in D.C. Do you want me to come back through here on Tuesday and pick you up on my way home?"

"No, I have to work up until the last minute. I'm planning to drive over from Norfolk late on Wednesday."

As they continued to talk, Katie stood uncertainly,

feeling a little out of place. She reached for a mug to pour Max a cup as well.

"So, Katie, I see you've met one of my younger brothers."

"Second in line and not near as important. At least that's what my big brother always taunted when we were younger." Nate laughed, looked over at Max, then grinned at Katie with a smile not unlike his older brother's.

"So there are more of you at home?" Katie asked as she pushed a strand of her hair behind her ear.

"Yes, Seth and Sam. They're twins."

"And always in trouble," Max chimed in with that devastating smile she hadn't seen in a while but which still made her heart leap in response.

Nate's laughter rang out in the small kitchen. "You know Sam is engaged to Becky?" he informed Max with a twinkle in his eyes.

"What? Why, that's great."

Katie clutched the mug between her hands and stared at Max, trying to grasp this picture he was presenting of himself. Not at all like the dictatorial man of late. More like the man she'd met in the tower all those weeks ago, twinkle-eyed and teasing. She had a sudden, overwhelming longing, a stirring for another chance to do things differently where Max was concerned. What young Jamey would have called a 'do over.'

"Well, let's go take a look at this house of yours before our coffee gets cold. Then we'll grab an early dinner before I head out," Nate told Max as he placed one hand on his brother's shoulder and led him toward the door.

"I still can't believe it. Sam and Becky." Max chuckled as they walked out of the cottage.

"Speaking of weddings, what about that girl you were so all fired up about?"

Katie found herself straining to catch Max's answer,

but they were already out the door and down the steps, the front door closing off his reply.

Katie walked over to the tower, wondering about the girl who had Max so 'fired up.' She had never seen him with anyone around Paige Point, so maybe he was dating someone in St. Michaels. When she entered the building, she was hit with the smell of paint fumes. She ran up the steps, stopping when she reached the painter.

"Excuse me." She had to raise her voice over the loud music coming from the man's radio. "Are you planning to paint this whole area?"

"Yes, miss, boss's orders."

"Don't paint over the heart, okay. It's ... from when I was a kid," she added with a sheepish smile.

"It's okay, Mike. Just cut around it."

Katie spun around at the sound of Max's voice. He and Nate were right below her. As they approached the landing, she stepped out of their way. Nate smiled and nodded as he followed Max up to the candle room. Katie watched the backs of both men as they walked away from her, unaware that she was comparing their broad shoulders and muscular thighs. Max won hands down.

A sudden gust of cold air swept into the cottage as Pop entered carrying an armful of logs for the fireplace. They'd just finished dinner, and Katie was setting up the Scrabble board on the coffee table. "Oh, let me help you with that, Pop."

"Move the screen, Katie."

Katie complied with his request, scurrying over to remove the screen just as Pop was bending over to release his burden. "Get the fire started while I bring in the rest."

Katie did as she was told, wadding up old newspaper, stuffing it in the grate. With a handful of kindling and several logs on top, she lit the paper, then ran to hold the door for Pop, who was on his last load.

"There, that should get us through the evening," he said in his familiar gravelly voice. He pulled up the high-back rocker and sat down, careful of his aching knees as he did so. "That was some good stew tonight, Katie. You're turning into a fine little cook."

Katie curled up on the chintz-covered, second-hand sofa. "Thanks, Pop."

"It's Friday night. Don't you have someplace to go? You're not thinking you have to stay with me, I hope. We can play Scrabble any evening. Why, even Max goes out over the weekend. I'm surprised you don't join him."

Katie laughed a little shakily, taking care how she answered him. "Are you trying to get rid of me?" she teased. She had taken great pains not to let Pop know of her prisoner-like circumstances and was afraid he would become suspicious as to why she seldom went anywhere. "Oh, you know me, Pop. I'd go out if I really wanted to, and as for Max, well, he's never asked me to join him. He's got his own friends I expect. Besides, he's out with his brother tonight." She grabbed one of the throw pillows on the sofa and held it against her chest. "Speaking of Max, have you seen him in town with anybody in particular lately?"

Pop began to rock back and forth with an ease of contentment. "Well, let's see, I've seen him with Tom having lunch over at the diner, and then Bessie and I saw him coming off the ferry last week with a some man, not anyone we knew, and let's see ..."

"No, I mean, in the female line."

Pop's eyes twinkled from under thick, bushy brows. "You mean a woman? Do I detect an interest there?"

She felt heat flash to her face. "Of course not."

Pop's eyebrows lifted as he continued to rock to and fro.

"I just heard he might be seeing someone, that's all," she said in her most flippant, indifferent tone. "Hey, how about a piece of hot apple pie?" She jumped up and ran into the kitchen, determined to change the subject. It wouldn't do to ask too many questions. Knowing Pop, he would probably ask Max outright about what they had just talked about.

After they ate their pie, they settled down in front of the Scrabble game board. About twenty minutes into the game, Pop built the word 'custody,' reminding Katie of the evening when Max had told her to look up the word, that she might learn something. Her eyes cut over to the dictionary they kept handy to check for correct spelling while playing the game. After her turn, in which she added the letters a-t-e to the d thus forming the word 'date', Katie picked up the dictionary while Pop sat thinking during his next turn.

Katie thumbed through the pages and quickly found the word. *Imprisonment* jumped off the page, hitting Katie right between the eyes. Irritated, she closed the book with a snap. For the next hour of play, that word on the game board seemed to mock her.

Pop soon decided to go to bed, leaving Katie with little to do at 9:30 on a Friday night. She quickly gathered up the game pieces and put the box away. She heard the cars from the late crew leave the compound, so, after piddling around, straightening a loose stack of magazines, and cleaning the dessert dishes, Katie decided to walk over to the keeper's house. She pulled on a heavy sweater and stepped outside, her skin tingled in the crisp night air. As she walked to the other house, she gazed up at the light, mesmerizingly brilliant as it repeatedly flashed its signature pattern.

She picked her way across the dormant ground and thought about how busy they had all been lately. After a pipe burst and flooded the main floor of the keeper's house, she and Pop had moved into the cottage temporarily while Max's crew worked to clean up and restore the damage. Although a major setback at the time, this gave Max the excuse he needed to renovate the entire first floor of the main house, which included the kitchen, the large, outdated bathroom, and the two bedrooms at the far end. Katie reached in and flipped the light switch, but it didn't work. So she tried the one next to it and the porch light flared, lighting up the steps.

Wishing she had thought to bring a flashlight, she entered the house, using the dull light from the porch to mark her steps across the foyer into the now-gutted kitchen. She carefully walked through to the high-ceilinged room, flipping switches as she went. Still no light. She was anxious to see the progress the stonemasons were making on their restoration of the original fireplace. These men were true craftsman. Max hired the best—that was for sure. It still amazed her how he'd gotten them here so quickly. She guessed it helped to be a wealthy property developer.

The moonlight allowed for ample viewing of the two back bedrooms that were being converted into a modern master suite with the addition of a bathroom and large walk-in closets. The combination of the historic with the contemporary, marrying the Old World charm of this fine old house with the latest in modern conveniences was like a re-birth. It made the work Katie had done earlier in the house more like a facelift, a lick and a promise, nothing like what was going on now. It was truly wonderful, the metamorphic change that was taking place here, changes she would never have been able to implement, not in her entire lifetime.

With an overwhelming sadness, Katie walked through the beautiful old house that had been home to real heroes of the sea. Men who'd spent hours scanning the surrounding waters for any sign of maritime distress. Men who'd daily climbed hundreds of steps checking oil levels and trimming the wicks. She grieved the loss of an era in history where flesh and blood tended the lights that were now automated and impersonal, many rendered useless due to satellites and computers. Now, who kept watch for the soul that was drowning? The light saved many, to be sure. It still stood vigil, but only to a point. The eyes of man were also needed. In the past they were an undeniable team, the keeper and the light. Both were critical, the keeper more so, for without him the light would go out, the oil would run dry, the foghorn would be silent. Forever the romantic, she grimaced. "Look where it's gotten me."

Katie wandered up the stairs, her hand sliding upward on the banister with each tentative step. On the landing, she paused to look out of the large, arched window. She could see the tower and the fourth order Fresnel lens bursting with light every four and a half seconds. A wave of loneliness engulfed her. She had become a prisoner in the place of her dreams, and the light now seemed to mock her as it marked her time of internment. She had so wanted to live here, to call this place home, but not like this. Suddenly disgruntled and unhappy, she turned and descended the steps. She was standing in the living room running her fingers along the front of the newly hand-carved mantle when she heard Max come in.

"Inspecting the work, I see."

Katie lowered her hands from the smooth wood. Max stood frighteningly austere with the porch light behind him casting his tall form in dark shadows. Even if he hadn't spoken, Katie would have known who he was. His stance and bearing had become so familiar to her these past weeks. The tilt of his head when he was going over elevation drawings, the way his mass of blond hair fell forward over one eye as he did so. The yellow, number-two pencil he held between his teeth when he sat at his computer, the way his face glowed with enthusiasm when he and Pop were talking about the past keepers of the light, the way the muscles in his arms rippled when he took a plane to an old piece of wood. All those images were safely tucked in her memory.

"Pop went to bed early, so I thought I'd take a quick walk-through." When he didn't comment, she added, somewhat sarcastically, "Don't worry, I'm not casing the joint, if that's what you're thinking."

Max walked slowly toward her. "I see three weeks in my *custody* hasn't mellowed that mouth of yours."

Oh Lord, there was that word again. Would it haunt her all evening? "I'm not in your custody."

"Don't be too sure of that, angel. There's more than one way of taming a little shrew."

"I am not a shrew. Please don't call me that."

"Please? Maybe this little time together has worked a miracle," he drawled.

Trying her best to ignore him, Katie asked, "Did you and Nate have a nice evening?"

"We did."

"Your brother seems nice."

"He is." He continued to step toward her.

Katie felt this sudden urge to run, but her feet took root in the floor like a new seedling. She stood there like a statue, clenching and unclenching her hands into fists.

Max reached out and pulled her toward him. Katie was unprepared for the assault on her senses as his firm lips claimed hers with a frightening intensity. She struggled silently, straining against his powerful grip as he held her tightly against his chest, demanding a response. A string of emotions ripped across her thoughts, leaving her defenseless against their onslaught. Powerless, Katie found herself swaying against him for support.

Max, evidently sensing the change, lessoned his grip and moved his arms around her, holding her firmly, but tenderly, against his broad frame. The pressure of his lips lessoned in their demand, moving instead with tender persuasion from her lips, to the side of her mouth, to her cheek. He made his way back to her parted lips before laying claim to them again. Pliant as putty in his hands, she melted against him, her hands moving upward with tentative, exploring fingers before coming to rest in a vice-like grip on his shoulders. Max lifted his head, leaving her trembling and breathless with longing.

"Katie." Max drew in a deep breath, then released her, gently sliding his hands down her arms before dropping them to his sides. Katie reached out with her right hand, gripping the mantle for support. Riveted to the spot, she stared up at him. Max rubbed his hand around the back of his neck, then took hold of her hand and led her across the floor and into the brisk night air. Once they were down the steps, he turned and stared at her before stuffing his hands in his pockets.

"Go to bed, Katie," he said, nodding his head toward the cottage, his expression rueful as he met her gaze. He offered a small smile. "It seems I've figured out a way to shut you up after all."

Katie blinked and clamped her lips together. Had she no self-control where he was concerned?

"Don't you ever touch me again, Max Sawyer."

"Unfortunately, it doesn't last very long," Max said as he removed his hands from his pockets to give her a gentle push toward the cottage.

Max lit a cheroot, exhaled a puff of smoke and watched as Katie entered the cottage. He gazed at the tip of the small cigar and took another draw. The faint glow from the porch light had allowed him to see the gamut of emotions that had crossed her face. He could tell she'd wanted him to kiss her. She'd stood tense and waiting while the pale light danced off her stormy blue eyes. Her soft parted lips and her golden hair had shimmered in the soft light, tousled and falling over her shoulders. She was beautiful.

He thought it'd be enough, just having her here. But it

wasn't. Seeing her in the mornings, in her flannel robe, while she scurried around making breakfast, made him realize what it would be like, married to her, building a life together. After he'd gotten her letter, that's what he'd come here to do—to set the record straight to who he was, to confront any and all issues concerning her aunt's accusations, and to give her the opportunity to get to know him—Max Sawyer. But then, he'd caught her stealing. And until he found out what that was about, he'd bide his time. He'd wait. He was good at waiting. After all, he'd waited years for her to grow up. Another month or two wouldn't matter.

Twenty minutes later, donned in her warm flannel pajamas, Katie lay snug under her quilt, her heart filled with a longing she could no longer deny. Max drew a passion from her she didn't know she possessed. When he kissed her, she melted like cold butter on hot toast. As she thought of how her heart had cried for him not to stop, she groaned out loud. For a moment, she thought their kiss had meant something to him as well, but his abrupt withdrawal puzzled her. Then, that damned twinkle had appeared in his eyes. She obviously amused him. She sighed. Her imprisonment went far deeper than she'd realized.

Katie turned onto her side. Unable to sleep, her thoughts were drawn to that night in the tower, after Davy's funeral. She had stopped crying and had lifted her head away from her sailor's chest to look up at his face, but it was shrouded in darkness. Just like Max's had been tonight. As she'd peered through the black night, he had leaned forward and brushed his lips against hers. Although brief and feather-light, the unexpectedness of it had caught her off guard. For a moment, her grief was stilled, and in that infinitesimal pause, hope filled its place.

She remembered how his head had jerked up, abruptly,

as if yanking back on self-imposed reins, quickly peeling her tightly clinging arms from around his waist as he rose to his feet.

"I'm sorry, I shouldn't have done that," he had said. "Forgive me. You'll be all right now." He'd spoken in a clipped, hurried tone.

At sixteen, Katie hadn't understood the complexity of the situation. Before she realized it, all that was left of the moment was the sound of his feet against the iron steps. Katie, who had never been kissed before, had come to call it her *quickening,* for in that moment her grieving, desperate soul moved from death to life. At the time she'd thought he had taken her heart to a place wild with longing. But the only wild longing she was experiencing was right now, this very minute, and if she wasn't careful, Max Sawyer would steal her heart.

Sleep continued to evade her. Normally when she couldn't sleep, she would just get up and paint. So why not now? After all, it was just a short walk to her aunt's house. She threw off the covers, quickly dressed, then slipped downstairs to the mudroom to get Buddy. "Hey, boy, are you ready for a little late-night adventure?" Buddy thumped his tail in reply, then they quietly exited through the back door.

## Chapter 12

Under the heavy weight of fatigue, Katie struggled to pull herself out of a deep sleep. Her eyelids possessed a will of their own and refused to open. But the constant prodding against her shoulder, which seemed to mirror the pounding in her temples, had her moaning and rolling over onto her side. Her eyes squeezed tightly against the glaring flash of light aimed at her face.

Katie made a halfhearted attempt to swat at the hand jabbing her shoulder before tugging the covers up over her head. That same firm hand snatched the quilt off her, prompting her to draw up her knees and try to cover her bare feet. Irritated, she peeked through sleepy lids and was met by the sight of a pair of lean thighs standing at the side of her bed. Her eyes widened as realization seeped through her fuzzy brain.

"We missed you at breakfast," drawled the deep voice above her head.

Katie blinked, then shot up onto one elbow. A pair of intense brown eyes stared down at her with impatience. She closed her eyes again and dropped back onto the bed to avoid the inevitable confrontation.

She'd lost track of time last night as she'd worked feverishly on her third painting, a strong cup of hot tea at her elbow. She'd faced the truth with courage and practicality. Except for Pop, everyone she loved was gone, and those she dreamed of loving were unattainable. So, oblivious to the late hour, she was driven like she never had been before, propelled by intensity and passion. She had no idea what time she'd gone to bed.

"Is your phone dead?" Max's reached into her thoughts, forcing her to open her eyes.

"Lily has been calling you the past hour. She finally got a hold of me, frantic that you might have had an accident."

"Saturday," she groaned as she sat up, placing her feet on the hooked rug.

"Are you sick, or something?" Max asked, sounding suspicious.

"Or something." She moaned, then gazed up at the powerful figure towering over her. "Would you mind?"

Max eyed her with a thoughtful expression, then strode from the room.

Katie showed up to work two hours late, casting Lily a sheepish look as she entered through the front door. Lily responded in her usual understanding manner by motioning Katie to the back. Taking in what Katie knew were dark circles and a haggard appearance, Lily soon had her sitting in the break room with a cup of coffee. "You look awful."

Katie sighed, then glanced over at her friend. "I'm really sorry, Lily. I just overslept."

"Why? Were you up all night?"

Katie looked back at her friend in a meaningful way, saying 'yes' without actually speaking the word out loud. "I've had to start staying up late to work on my paintings. Otherwise, I would never get them done. But listen, Pop and Max don't know anything about it, and I want to keep it that way, okay?"

"All right," Lily said with a slight question in her green eyes. "Finish your coffee, and we'll do a little inventory."

Later, while they counted screwdrivers, Lily asked, "So where have you been? Except for Saturdays, we never see you."

The doorbell chimed as a customer entered.

"You know what they say about all work and no play?"

While Lily paused to jot down a number on her pad, Katie searched desperately for a reply.

"My thoughts exactly, Lily."

Katie's hand stilled on a screwdriver at the sound of Max's voice.

"She has been working too hard. As a matter of fact, I'm planning on taking Katie out tonight."

Katie felt her eyes widen and her jaw drop.

Max placed his fingers under her chin, shutting her mouth. "So, Katie, I'll pick you up after work tonight. We'll go have dinner and maybe take in a movie. Nothing fancy, so you won't need to change," he said, his eyes locking onto hers.

"But—"

"No excuses," he quickly interrupted.

Katie was certain his engaging smile was solely for Lily's benefit.

"Angus agrees, in case you were wondering," Max continued. "He seems to think like the rest of us that you have been overdoing it lately."

Katie searched for any indication he could be mocking her, but found none.

"That does sound nice," Lily said, glancing over at her with an encouraging smile. "Don't worry, Max. She'll be ready."

That evening, Katie sat across from Max at Tina's Spaghetti House, doing her best to stifle another yawn. She'd worked straight through the day with Lily, not having had a chance to catch a nap.

"You haven't eaten much," Max observed, twirling spaghetti around his fork.

"I told you not to order so much food." Almost three-quarters of the serving of meatballs and spaghetti remained on her plate. "I'm not a big eater."

Thinking of last night's kiss had Katie looking everywhere but at Max's face. Her fingers played along the edge of the white napkin in her lap as she searched her fatigued-filled brain for something to break the embarrassing silence. "So you've been gone a lot lately."

"Do you miss me?" he asked with a slight grin.

"Not particularly."

Max sat back, lifted his wine glass and appeared to be studying the rich burgundy legs trailing down the sides. "I'm having a problem with one of my clients. He's highly particular about the original art placed in his hotels, and unfortunately I'd convinced him to use an artist who is now no longer available. I've had a series of meetings with the man, trying to get him to consider another option, but his particular idiosyncrasies make him a pain in the neck to work with ... so it's been difficult."

Katie's ears perked up at the word "art." "And did you ... convince him?" she asked with real interest, stifling a yawn.

"I think so. He's thinking about it at least."

He smiled across at her, and lulled by the affable moment, Katie's treacherous heart leapt in response.

"What kind of art?"

"Landscapes." He took a sip of his wine. "Stunning, if I do say so myself." He set the wine glass on the table and indicated her plate with a nod. "Well, if you're sure you're finished, I'll get the check."

Landscapes. That explained why the customer was so particular. There were so many styles that a simple variation could change the whole tone of a painting. It's why she loved them.

Later, while sitting beside Max in The Pitt Theatre, it was all Katie could do to stay awake. Once a month they played retro films. Tonight's feature was *Goldfinger*. Any other time a James Bond flick would have held her attention. But not this evening. Once during the film Max nudged her with his elbow and told her that she was missing the best part. Katie sat up straighter but soon found herself slumped back against the seat. Blinking as the house lights came up, she noticed the credits rolling up the large screen in front of her. She pulled herself out of her chair and stumbled down the aisle, causing Max to place a steadying hand under her elbow. On the drive home, her battle to fight off fatigue failed miserably as she tried to stifle yawn after yawn.

Once inside the cottage, Katie paused before going up the stairs, feeling like she had to say something. "I'm sorry I fell asleep."

"Was it me, or the movie?"

"Neither."

"Well, that's a relief," he said. "But it's just ten o'clock. Sometimes a lack of sleep points to a guilty conscience. Anything you'd like to tell me?"

"All right, so I had a short night last night. Is that a crime?"

"With you, it probably is. Maybe I should check my watch and cufflink collection?" The sardonic look in his eyes held an unbending expression.

To Katie's horror, a sudden rush of tears filled her eyes. Fearful they would spill over, she turned and rushed up the stairs.

"Katie, wait!" He started toward the foot of the stairs. Had those been tears in Katie's eyes? Hell, he'd only wanted to egg her on, see if she'd tell him the truth about why she'd stolen his hardware. But he'd never expected her to cry.

"Ahem." Angus stood in the kitchen doorway, his bushy eyebrows arched in question.

"Angus." Max stopped. "What are you doing up? Are

you all right?"

"Just a bit of indigestion. On my way back to bed now." He nodded toward the landing. "You know, in my day, it was a sad thing to be bringing home a lass in tears."

Max ran his hand along the back of his neck. "You're right. I was boorish and rude."

"Katie is a mite high-strung. Full of energy, that girl." Angus smiled. "My sweet Emma and I never could have children. I remember the day Katie started calling me Pop, officially adopting me as her grampa. She was eleven. It was just her and her brother, then. A fine lad he was, too, until he was killed."

Yes, Davy had been a fine man. A great friend, a beloved brother. Remorse swept through Max. And Davy's sister deserved better.

"Well, I'm off. Have a great Thanksgiving." Max shook hands with Angus.

"We will, son, and you, too."

Katie wouldn't look at him. Max could hardly blame her since he treated her like a plebe under his command. He felt like a heel for the way he'd handled things last night. But truth be known, she worried him. Had things gotten that bad for her? He could only imagine what it must be like to be orphaned. To have lived above a store in a one-room apartment, but that wouldn't cause a person of character to steal. What she took was practically worthless. It didn't make sense. Unless she did it strictly as sabotage.

"Katie, would you please walk with me to the car?"

Katie followed Max outside and watched silently as he tossed his duffle into the back seat before turning to her.

"Listen, I didn't mean to hurt you last night. I've tried to make sense of why you stole from me but frankly, I can't."

"I know." She avoided his gaze. "It was a stupid prank.

It was silly and childish. But, you need to know this, I would do that and more, to keep you from turning the station into one of your spas," Katie said, pinning him with her intense gaze.

"Well, I guess forewarned is forearmed," he said lightly. Somehow sabotage didn't seem the right answer.

When she didn't respond, he climbed in his car and shut the door.

Max turned out of the driveway onto the street. So, she still thought he was turning the station into a resort. A slight smile tugged at the corners of his mouth. Good, that should keep her around a while, even if it was just to fight with him.

The following week progressed along the same lines as the previous ones. Katie worked during the day, played board games with Pop during the evenings and, when she could, slipped out to work on her paintings, careful not to be gone too long or stay up too late. The last thing she needed was another disaster-filled evening with Max. To say he was suspicious was putting it mildly. Every time she looked in his direction, she caught him watching her with the contemplative "specimen under glass" look he seemed to reserve just for her.

December 1$^{st}$ came in with a torrent of rain. After breakfast, Max left for a meeting in St. Michaels. As soon as he was out of sight, Katie tugged on her yellow rain slicker and slipped out to work on her fifth painting. It was of the St. Augustine Light, which, except for a few final touches, was almost finished. On her way back to the cottage to prepare lunch, she called Falcon Designs, leaving the same message as before. She grew more and more discouraged when she received no call back, but she couldn't risk not doing the paintings in case they were truly busy, not just ignoring her.

Late that afternoon, Max finally drove into Paige Point, forgoing the ferry after his conference call went longer than expected. He left St. Michaels after another frustrating meeting with his assistant. They had spent an hour on the phone with Peter Markesan, the royal pain in the neck, as well as a few other places. It took some work, but Peter reluctantly agreed to use the new artist.

Max's cell phone interrupted his thoughts as he got a call from Lily telling him that his order had arrived. Minutes later, he arrived at the store.

"My, that was quick," Lily said.

"I was literally about to pass by here when you called."

"Good, your order is right over here."

Max leaned his hip against the counter as Lily opened the box in front of him.

"Here you go. I'm sorry it's taken so long." She paused when she saw the contents. "Ten toilet plungers."

"What?" Max pulled the box toward him, mouth gaping, eyes narrowed in confusion.

"I take it this is not what you wanted?"

"I didn't order these. I ordered faucet handles."

Lily opened the fat manual. "Let's take a look-see and compare order numbers. Looks like they are just one letter off. See, the handles end in a lowercase j and the plungers in an i. I see Tom placed the order. I'll have to speak to him about this," she said in a teasing manner. "But seriously, I'm really sorry, Max. Were you in a hurry for these? Are you fixing up another place?"

"They were originally for the cottage, but now I'm planning to use them in the keeper's house."

"I just wondered because Katie's already replaced those in the cottage."

"I'm sorry?"

Lily glanced up as she typed in the correct order. "The hardware, Katie's replaced all of it in the cottage and had started on the keeper's house, too, I think. Knobs, hinges, handles, you name it. You should have seen the fuss she made over the doorknobs. They had to match the originals perfectly, so we had to search for a special company that specialized in reproductions. Hence, this catalogue." She patted her hand on the cover as she spoke. But at the look on his face she said, "Didn't you know?"

"No, I didn't." But Lily sure had filled in some blanks.

"Oh dear, I hope I haven't given anything away? I thought that's why you invited them to move in with you. I thought you knew."

"So you're telling me that Katie replaced all of the hardware in the cottage? That she bought and paid for them?"

Lily nodded. "That, and a few other things."

Dumfounded, he asked, "Is there anything else I should know?"

"Yes, but don't look at me for answers. I'm going to be in trouble as it is. You'll have to talk to Katie if you have any more questions."

"Oh, I fully intend to." Max placed the credit card on the counter and at Lily's questioning look, he said, "For the plungers. Our little Miss Kate is going to need all ten before I'm through with her." Then at Lily's raised brows, he added, "We've had a battle going on, and it's time for the showdown."

"Oh, dear." Lily's eyes lit up with mirth. "As bad as that."

"Worse."

Lily handed over his sales receipt. "You know there is something I'd like to say in her defense."

"Afraid she won't have any hide left when I'm through?"

Lily gave him one of her knowing smiles and said with confidence, "You wouldn't hurt her."

He grinned back. "No, but she's sure going to think I

will. So what did you want to tell me?"

"Just that Katie has been through a lot over the past five or six years. Amazingly, she always seems to recover. She's taken some hard hits during that time. Losing her parents, then her brother. And God only knows how she lived with that bitter aunt of hers. I'm so thankful Angus was there. One thing I've realized, though, is that each hit has taken longer to get over than the one before. And this last hit, well, it was pretty hard." Lily paused for a second, then added, "You know, she gave up a full scholarship to one of the finest schools in this country, just to take care of an old man she's not even related to. Oh, she's impulsive and mischievous, and at times acts more like a fourteen-year-old boy than a twenty-one-year-old young woman, but she has a great heart, and I'd sure hate to see it get broken."

Max laid his hands on each side of the box. "Thank you. Now at least a few critical pieces have fallen into place." As Lily's eyebrows pinched together, he reached over, gave Lily's shoulders a quick squeeze, then asked, "This last *hit,* could you tell me about it?"

"I'm afraid not."

"I respect that." But he wasn't happy about it. He wanted to know everything about Katie. Understand what made her tick.

Once outside, Max placed the box of plungers in the front passenger seat. He closed the door and walked down the street, hands stuffed in the pockets of his slacks. He shifted his shoulders as the lunch crowd passed him on the sidewalk, then entered Paul's Deli. He spotted Tom at the lunch counter.

"Mind if I join you?" Max asked.

Peggy placed a hamburger and fries in front of Tom, then turned to Max.

"I'll have the pasta special and iced tea."

"Your order came in this morning," Tom said.

"I know. I just picked it up."

Peggy returned with Max's hot plate special.

"Tom. Where did all of that furniture come from? In the cottage and keeper's house? Did it belong to the Kendrick family?"

"You mean you don't know?" Tom sank his teeth into the hamburger.

"If I did, I wouldn't be asking."

"It's Katie's, the whole kit and caboodle. Well, at least, until you bought the place. I thought that's why you had them move in with you. I thought you knew."

Thirty minutes later, Max strode with purpose back to his car.

And all this time, he'd thought Katie was a thief. No wonder she'd called *him* one. A change of tactics was definitely now in order.

Katie looked up as Max placed the box down in front of her. She'd spent the morning at the cottage comparing a couple bids for some replacement windows needed for the keeper's house.

"Seems there was a mix up in one of my orders," he stated with a peculiar look in his eye that Katie found disturbing. "I thought you might find an appropriate use for those." His blond head nodded toward the box.

Pretty certain what she would find inside, Katie lifted the cardboard flaps and there, staring up at her were ten toilet plungers.

"I ... I have no idea what to do with all of these." She pushed them back toward him. "You should have just left them. Lily can send them back or sell them."

"Who said I got those from Lily?"

Katie's mouth clamped shut, while she waited for him

to continue. Seconds ticked by, and her heart began to pound. Suddenly, Max turned away, his long strides taking him to the door. He turned back toward her. "I'll be gone for the next four or five days. Think you can cope with everything while I'm gone?"

She nodded then Max turned and strode out of the cottage. She let out the breath she hadn't realized she'd been holding. She'd been given a reprieve. But for how long?

The next day, Katie was just about to fix a pot of tea for her and Pop when Nate appeared at the door.

"Back already?" Katie handed him a hot cup.

"Yea, Max thought I should take a look over the site."

"I'm so ready to be done with all of the dust," she said as they walked together throughout the downstairs area.

"This last minute stuff always takes longer because of the detailed work of the finishing carpenters and the painters," Nate explained to Katie. "It is a messy business. I thought Max should have waited a while before he refurbished this place. Although it was in pretty good condition when he started. Someone had obviously kept the place up over the years."

Katie smiled at the compliment Nate had not realized he had just given.

"He sure is in an all-fired hurry to finish this place, though."

"So, how many properties does Max have?"

"Oh gosh, Max owns about ten elite hotels and inns across the United States. M.F.S. Enterprise also finds and develops properties in conjunction with other hotel firms. But that's just a part of the business. Max just recently acquired the controlling interest in The Bayside Inn."

"But that's right near here in St Michaels."

"I know. Max has his own suite of rooms there. Didn't you know?"

"No."

"Oh yeah, he's been staying there on and off for the past several months. I actually stay there as well if I have to spend the night. It's one of the reasons why I can't understand why he wanted this old placc so much," Nate said as he ran his hand over a section of drywall.

"I had no idea."

"Yep. Of course, you obviously know about his design firm since you're one of his designers."

"Actually," she said, completely floored at what she was hearing, "I don't have a clue what you're talking about."

"Really, so you must be freelance then. I've never known him to use anyone outside his firm before so you must really be one talented individual."

*More like slave labor*. Katie just smiled and tilted her head toward him in a gesture of thanks. "So why do you think he's put such a rush on this property?" Katie asked, her curiosity getting the better of her.

Nate threw her a grin and said, "No earthly clue, unless it has something to do with his mystery woman."

"Really. I didn't know he was dating anyone," she said as nonchalantly as she could.

"Neither did we until Thanksgiving. But that's not to say he hasn't had his share of female company. They have all gone for my big brother, let me tell you.

"So how did that make you and Seth and Sam feel? Were you ever jealous?"

Nate laughed heartily. "No way. They all had younger sisters." He gave Katie a wicked wink.

Katie bubbled up with laughter, and realized she hadn't laughed like that in weeks.

By Saturday, Max still had not returned.

While straightening up some boxes of Christmas ornaments, Katie felt someone tugging on her shirtsleeve. Turning, she was met with Jamey's glowing face and incorrigible grin. Katie threw her arms around him and received a great big hug in return.

"Jamey! It has been weeks since I've seen you. How is school and soccer?"

"They're okay." Then, not one to waste words, he asked, "When are we going on our date, Katie?"

Jamey looked up at her with such darling appeal that Katie found his heartfelt request hard to resist. "How about tonight? That is, if you don't already have other plans for the evening."

"Nope, tonight's perfect."

"What about tonight?" his mother asked as she walked up to them.

"Katie and I are going on our date tonight," he burst out, jumping up and down with excitement.

"Really, on such short notice? Jamey, are you sure you haven't coerced Katie in some way?"

"What does co ... cowersed mean?"

"It means to make someone do something they may not want to do."

Katie laughed, and said, "No, he hasn't. It was my idea, actually. So what do you say, Mom? Can he come?"

"Well, if you're sure you don't mind ..."

"She doesn't mind, Mom." Jamey's eager response had them both laughing. After settling on a time, Katie waved at them as they left the store.

Katie changed into a hot pink outfit she still had in her closet upstairs at Rods n' Reels. She hadn't worn it since last winter and had forgotten how bright and cheery it was, perfect for a hot date with a nine-year-old. The pants were rosewood-colored cords, and she matched it with a bright, long-sleeve orange cashmere cardigan then topped it off with a vibrant raspberry pea coat. She pulled part of her hair back with a shiny barrette so her face was uncovered except for the occasional spray that escaped from the clip. After slipping on her warm Uggs, she walked down the block to Tina's.

The exuberant Jamey laughed and chatted happily during their meal together, and Katie smiled at him in return. At one point when Katie looked up from her plate, she caught him gazing at her with the adoring eyes of a young puppy. She winked back at him, which broke the spell and caused him to grin.

While the waitress cleaned off their dinner plates to make way for dessert, Katie sat in the booth waiting for Jamey to return from the restroom, periodically glancing back and forth between an app on her phone and the front entrance. Glancing up, she saw to her horror that Max had entered the restaurant and was in the process of holding out a chair for a slender brunette. Katie felt there was something familiar about her. She was tastefully dressed in a sleek fitting blue dress and heels. She couldn't see the woman's face but figured anybody with a body like hers probably had the face to match. He would date someone like that. As Max stepped toward his own chair, Katie, eyes widening, snatched up the menu and held it up in front of her face. He would be in a position to stare right at her. She slid her body as far down in the seat as she could.

"Do you actually think that I wouldn't notice you sitting over here? Don't you have work to do?" the deep tones of the all-too-familiar voice asked.

Katie looked up at him from over the top of the menu before slamming it shut with a snap. "I'll get to the paper work after dinner, if it's all right with you. Besides, you were gone, and Pop was out with Bessie, so I decided to have dinner out before I went back to the cottage," she said defensively, feeling ridiculous at having been caught hiding behind a menu.

A gleam of speculation lit Max's eyes and a slow smile spread across his handsome features.

"By yourself?"

"Yes." She glanced toward the restroom before returning her gaze to his.

"May I join you?" he asked.

"No, you may not. Besides, you have a date. And I want to be alone, if you don't mind."

"Looks like the table's set for two to me."

Rolling her eyes, she said, "So I have a date. Now will you go before he comes back?"

He smiled at her. "That all depends, since you're my *responsibility.*"

Blast him. He could be aggravating.

"I feel that I should at least meet your mystery man." Max sat on the bench seat, sliding himself comfortably in across from her.

Katie's eyes sparkled dangerously. "That is not necessary, and you know it."

"Well, he must be someone special in order for you to disobey my orders." He smiled, infuriating her even more.

Katie raised her chin in defiance. "He is wonderful!"

"And?" Max encouraged her to continue.

Katie leaned toward him, taking up the challenge. "First and foremost, he treats me with respect. He's polite, handsome, charming, *and* he adores me. As a matter of fact, he has asked me to marry him. And believe me, if things were different I would, too, just to get away from you."

The look of complete surprise on Max's face had Katie inwardly smirking in triumph. She watched as his eyes narrowed into slits. He frowned for a moment, until something caught his attention from across the room. "And is he about four feet tall?"

Katie swung around to see Jamey approaching them.

She groaned inwardly, then slumped forward. With elbows on the table, she placed her chin in her hands.

"Hi, Max. What are you doing here?" Jamey asked with enthusiasm.

Max's brown eyes crinkled down at his young friend, his grin broadening at Jamey's happy, upturned face. "Just saying hello."

"Katie and I are on a date."

"I know. She told me."

"Would you like to join us?" Jamey asked in his most polite, gentlemanly manner.

Max's lips twitched, but he answered seriously. "Thank you, Jamey, but I have a date as well, so you two enjoy yourselves." He slipped out of the booth, then headed back across the room to take his seat opposite the dark-haired, very attractive woman.

Katie watched with envy as he leaned toward the woman with that devastating smile of his. He glanced over at her and winked, before giving his attention back to *his* mystery date.

## Chapter 13

Katie strolled, Buddy at her side, across the dormant grass. When she woke that morning to go to church, she had discovered that Max hadn't returned last night. Visions of Max with his dark-haired mystery gal bombarded her. Her heart sank at the thought that he must have taken her back to the hotel last night. Then she pulled herself up short. Why in heaven's name should she care about that? Max Sawyer was annoying and insufferable and whoever this mystery girl was, well, she was welcome to him. Let him wield his highhanded ways with her instead.

Katie left the property and spent the next hour in the attic of her aunt's house looking for the old-fashioned multi-colored Christmas lights. Once found, she stuffed them in two large brown paper bags and carried them outside. Dressed in black jeans, a black cape, and a pair of long cabled gloves, she knew looked like she had stepped from the pages of a fashion magazine instead of the local discount mart where she, with Jill's help, had pulled the entire outfit together.

Bessie, who had been spending most of her time over the weekends at the light station, met her at the door with a steaming mug of hot chocolate topped with plump tiny marshmallows.

"Oooo, thank you," Katie said, accepting the mug after depositing the heavy bags on the floor.

Pop was just finishing his clam chowder and asked, "Katie, how was your evening out last night?"

"Oh, it was fun." *Until Max showed up.* "Jamey is such a great kid."

"Max arrived just as Bessie and I were coming in. He had a date with him."

"He brought her here?" Angus stared at her in an odd way, which made her realize she'd revealed too much with her tone. "I mean, he brought home a date?"

"He did, and when he discovered you weren't home from work yet, he seemed mighty put out about it. I assured him that you were all right and had only decided to stay in town for dinner before coming home. He seemed fine with that until I told him you had a date. I had no sooner said that when he and Sal were back out the door to have dinner in town as well."

So that was her name. "So Pop, what was Sal like?"

"Oh, quite a lovely darlin', beautiful, too. Sal and Bessie got on real well for the short while she and Max were here. I can see why Max would like her. They seemed to have a real comfortable way with each other, like he's known her for years. Maybe she's the woman you heard about?"

"Umm, maybe," she responded.

Pop smiled and stood up from the table a little more feebly than normal. He steadied his tall, aging limbs on the back of the kitchen chair for just a moment before slowly walking into the sitting room where he, just as slowly, lowered his frame into the upholstered chair holding onto the side arms for support. Katie watched him in concern before turning toward Bessie with an unspoken question in her eyes.

"He'll be fine, dear," she whispered. "It's just taking him a little longer than usual to get around today."

Bessie ladled out an ample supply of clam chowder for Katie then went to join Angus by the fire. Katie stared at the huge portion before her, took four bites, then discreetly held the bowl down near the floor for Buddy to finish, careful to keep a watchful eye on Bessie in the next room. In seconds, he had licked the bowl clean. She jumped up and placed the bowl in the sink before anyone was the wiser.

"I'm going back outside," she yelled. Then closing the door behind her, she said under her breath, "For a hamburger."

Katie climbed the ladder with lights in hand, then began stringing them around the doorframe and the square columns stationed on each side of the front steps. Next, she draped the greenery over the top of the door, leaving enough so that equal amounts hung freely down on both sides. Stepping off the porch, she let out a contented sigh. She leaned the ladder against the gray dwelling, making sure it was secure before mounting the rungs. Thankfully, the metal hooks were still in place from the previous year. With the lights coiled together over one arm, she slowly unwrapped a portion of the strand then began looping on the lights. This rhythm of looping and climbing the ladder went on for about half an hour before she reached the more difficult section of the house where the roofline pointed up in a forty-five-degree angle. She was on the highest rung she dared go and was straining as she reached up on tiptoe to loop the strand up and over the hook when suddenly she felt the ladder move. Heart pounding, she glanced toward the ground. Max slowly ascended each rung.

Not daring to move, she'd surely be hurt if she fell from this height, she stood riveted near the top.

"Steady," he said from behind her. She felt the pressure of his lean body against the entire length of her back. Startled, she glanced back at him, her hair lightly brushing against the strong line of his jaw before meeting a pair of brown eyes slightly squinting against the bright winter sun. His left arm came around her and grabbed hold of the ladder while his right arm reached up beside hers, taking the strand of lights from her fingers and easily looping it over the hook above their heads.

"I thought I told you to stay off the ladder." He spoke near her ear, his tone light and teasing.

"I thought you meant the rickety one. This one is new." Her heart had started racing the moment he leaned up against her and was now going double time. A wave of shyness came over her. Max slipped the strand off her shoulder and pulled a few feet into his hand, then proceeded to loop another strand onto the next hook then the next. The last one was some distance away, so Max leaned even closer, causing her heart to thud wildly. The feel of him against her was sheer heaven, and the pounding of her heart rushed over her like a tidal wave in a storm. Max gazed down at her with eyes that told her he knew exactly the effect he was having on her, the slow tilt to his lips revealing all she needed to know. Max stepped down to the ground, then plucked her off the rungs, ignoring her protests in the process.

Overcome by her inner turmoil, Katie brushed at her clothes as if she had been rolling in the grass. She only stopped when Max placed a long finger under her chin, forcing her to look up at him.

"Shall we continue? There's still a few more feet to go," he playfully taunted as he moved the ladder farther along the front of the cottage, securing it against the top of the house. When Katie didn't move, he placed one foot on the bottom rung, then looked back at her over his shoulder. "Not quitting now, are you?" At the shake of her head, he asked, "Then hand me the rest of the lights and go inside and fix us a hot cup of anything. It's freezing out here."

Katie handed him the lights, then ran inside to make them a cup of hot chocolate. By the time she came out the front door, Max had not only finished the job but had also hoisted the ladder up and over his shoulder and was striding toward the storage shed. Katie stood on the lawn and watched him as he opened the shed door and with ease that probably came from years of strength training, he lowered the ladder in one lithe movement before propping it up against the wall. Katie couldn't help but notice his broad chest and shoulders and the slight swinging of his muscular arms as he walked toward her. As he neared, Katie handed him his hot cocoa.

Taking the mug from her gloved hands, he cast his eyes over the multi-colored lights. "So you like this gaudy look, do you?"

"The gaudier, the better," she responded.

He eyed her as they both sipped on the sweet, hot liquid, simultaneously licking their upper lips to remove any trace of melted marshmallow. Then before she knew what he intended, Max leaned forward and placed his warm mouth against her top lip in a tender kiss. "You missed some," he said with a hovering smile. He walked over to plug the cords into the outlets on the porch. "Well, shall we turn them on?"

A slight fluttering sensation moved in her stomach. "No, not yet, it's not dark."

"So?"

"It's tradition."

"Tradition? I thought this was the first time in years this place has seen any Christmas lights?"

"I ... actually have hung lights here before. Someday, I'm going to hang lights on the tower as well." Katie stopped abruptly when she realized what she'd said. "I've already tested them, and the lights all work if that's what you're worried about."

"Angel, I'm not *worried* about anything ... except for maybe you," he said quietly, tapping the end of her nose with his index finger. "Have it your way." He headed inside, and after a moment, she followed him.

Katie had slow-cooked a rump roast for dinner, adding chopped carrots and cubed potatoes to the pan during the last hour. Bessie and Max visited in the parlor while she worked. She looked up to find Pop hovering in the doorway and grinned. "Get the others, Pop. It's ready," she said as she pulled the hot wheat rolls from the oven. They all ate heartily, including Angus, for which Katie was thankful, considering his slow movements at lunchtime. She smiled fondly at him as he attacked his favorite meal. He had always been a meat and potatoes man, even with all of the fabulous fresh seafood in the area.

After putting the leftovers away, Katie peered out the window, then turned to summon the others. "Okay, it's time. Everybody, come on." She motioned for Pop, Bessie, and Max to come outside. When they all gathered in the front lawn, Katie told Max he could now do the honors. Max plugged in the lights, and instead of the blaze of the modern white lights so many people used this time of year, the cottage became aglow with all of the warmth of a Thomas Kinkaid painting. Red, blue, orange, and green smiled a welcome to all with old-fashioned holiday spirit.

Max started to speak, but Katie raised a finger to her lips to signal they weren't done yet. He raised his eyebrows, folded his arms across his chest, and watched as she and Angus smiled at each other as they began to sing. "Silent night, holy night ..."

Katie adjusted her alto voice to provide harmony to Pop's deep baritone, which carried the main melody. While they sang, she moved to Pop's side, receiving a feeble arm over her shoulder as she did so. Angus, although frail in body, was much stronger in voice.

When they finished, not a word was spoken. Then Bessie broke the silence with, "That was lovely, you two. I never tire of hearing you sing that. I look forward to it every Christmas."

"That was truly wonderful." Max gave her a curious look.

Katie felt her insides warm. Had she managed to surprise the unflappable Max Sawyer?

The next day, Max surprised them with a Frazier fir already mounted in a stand and ready for decorating.

"It's beautiful, Max." Katie leaned into the green needles and inhaled deeply. "Hey, let's have a party to decorate it. You know, a tree-trimming party. Bessie will help, and Tom and Lily will come as well, and then there's Jill and Jamey, of course." She licked her lips and asked casually, "What about you? Do you have anyone special you'd like to ask?" Her breath caught as she waited for his reply, hoping he wouldn't suggest the beautiful woman from the restaurant.

Max darted keen eyes in her direction and seemed about to say something before hesitating. "Sure. I'll think about it and let you know."

She ignored the stab of disappointment and planted a smile on her face. "Let's see, we'll need some decorations for this beauty." She ran her hands over the green needles, releasing the fragrant pine scent. "I know there's a bunch in the attic at Aunt's Margaret's."

She made a face at Max. "That is, if I have your *permission,*" she said, stressing the word for his benefit, "to go over there and get them."

"I think that could be arranged. I'm sure the carpenters can survive without you," he replied in smooth tones. "Especially since you've been slipping out for some time now."

"How could you possibly know that?" She folded her arms across her chest. "I only leave when you're not here."

"I thought as much." His tawny eyes held an unexpected laugher.

Katie raised her chin defiantly, then bubbled up with laughter. "How could you *not* know with only four hundred people in town?"

Max grinned at her, and for a moment their eyes met in pure comradeship.

"Seriously, though, has it affected my work? No, it has

not. I've done everything you've asked, and then some. And, I'm tired of walking everywhere, too."

"What's wrong with your Jeep?"

"As if you don't know."

He looked at her, clearly confused.

"You have my keys."

"What, these?" he asked as he pulled them from his pocket. "All you had to do was ask."

Katie crossed her arms across her chest again.

"Now let's go," he said as he strode to the door.

"Where?"

"Aunt Margaret's," he said over his shoulder.

"Hold up. I have to grab something. I want to make a quick stop at the church while we're out."


Aunt Margaret's attic was cold and smelly, and after about twenty minutes of opening boxes, Katie finally found the tree decorations underneath several heavy boxes filled with quilting material.

"I didn't know fabric could weigh so much," Katie said as she helped move the boxes to the floor. It took about fifteen minutes to carry the decorations down the steps to the hallway. They spent the next half hour going through the boxes, only taking out what they thought they'd need for the tree before consolidating the items into four of the boxes. After loading her Jeep, Max suggested they go get a bite to eat.

"Any suggestions?" he asked as they drove from the house.

Katie glanced down at her dust-laden clothes and grimaced. "I wouldn't even go into Paul's looking like this."

Max looked at his own clothing. "Hmm, I see your point. I have an idea, if you're game." He darted his eyes in her direction.

What the heck? She was enjoying her time with Max. "I'm game."

Max followed Katie's directions as he drove them through town, the evidence of Christmas everywhere with multi-colored lights on most of the houses and shops. They drove by the manger scene at the church, where Katie's parents and brother were buried.

"Pull up here. I'll just be a minute," she said.

Max cut the engine, stepped out of the vehicle, and watched Katie as she pushed open the gate that led to the historic church cemetery. He slowly followed, careful to keep a respectful distance. She whispered something, before squatting to place the little nut cake at the base of the headstone.

His gut churned at her action. How was he ever going to tell her? Since he'd been back, he'd relived the accident a hundred times. The boy on the bike, who'd come out of nowhere. The stench of burning rubber as he slammed on the breaks. If that tree hadn't have been there—but it was. As many times as he'd gone over it, he knew without a doubt, he would have still reacted the same way. And if Davy had been behind the wheel, he would have done the same thing.

Katie rose, then took a few steps to where Max was standing.

"You know that old maple tree that sits in the curve of Route 333?"

He nodded.

"That's where Davy was killed. Every time I pass that tree, I'm bombarded with questions. Would he be married now? Would I be an aunt?" She glanced back at the grave and shook her head. "I always wondered how something so majestic and so beautiful could be an accomplice in such a horrendous act."

Although, it only lasted a second, he caught a glimpse of loss and sadness on her lovely face. A sucker punch would have been less painful than that look. Because he'd put it there. He was responsible.

"Katie, I'm so sorry. I—"

"Don't be. Davy was one of the most joyful people I ever knew. Today is his birthday."

She smiled up at him and his heart lurched. He led Katie back to her Jeep. "That was a strange-looking cake you left there."

"Peanut butter and nuts."

"What kind of a birthday cake is that?"

Katie laughed. "It's for the squirrels."

A few minutes later, out on the highway, Katie noticed the signs and asked, "We're going to St. Michaels?"

"You'll see," he said with a smile. Twenty minutes later, he pulled up to the St. Michael's marina. He took her hand in his, relishing the feel of her soft skin encased in his, then led her to his surprise.

"What is it?" Katie asked, her mouth slightly open as she ran her hand along the high gloss teak railing of his pride and joy.

"It's a Uniesse."

"Ooo-nee-ess-ee," Katie repeated the name slowly, making sure she had the correct pronunciation.

"That's right, you got it. Take a look around, clean up if you want while I pull something together."

By the time Katie had returned, looking all fresh, he'd already prepared a savory dish of pasta with shrimp in a creamy white sauce with steamed asparagus on the side. Max grinned at Katie's obvious amazement. "Don't look so impressed. My chef prepares dishes like this for my freezer, so all I have to do is pop them in the microwave or the oven."

Katie took the steaming, succulent dish Max held out to her and carried it over to the table already set with silver and crystal. Max poured her a glass of Beaujolais Nouveau. "It's a light-bodied red wine."

"What does that mean?"

"Fewer tannins, therefore more palatable for someone who doesn't drink much." He smiled, then held the glass up in a salute to Katie before taking a sip.

Katie felt heat rush to her face, then followed suit while Max shared a few other interesting wine facts with her. He really could be quite charming.

Twirling her wine glass to see the 'legs' of the red cover the inside of the glass fascinated her, and on her third twirling, she glanced up to see Max regarding her with some amusement. Immediately placing the glass down on the table, she asked, "How is your research coming with Pop?"

He hesitated, then said, "You mean he hasn't been regaling you with Page Point Lighthouse lore?"

She shook her head.

"Well, it seems that Angus and I are related."

"Related? How?"

"Well, as you know, the keepers at Paige Point Light were from one family line with the exception of two, Angus being one of those. As it turns out, my family is related to the McAfee line."

"That's amazing."

How could Pop have shared that with Max, a total stranger, yet never said anything to her?

Her hurt must have shown on her face because Max said, "Don't be upset that Angus hasn't told you anything yet. We're still doing some detailed research, and he's probably wanting to gather all of the information first, knowing him."

Katie licked her lips, then met his gaze. "Is that why you bought the light station?"

"It's ... one reason, yes."

"Are you planning to live there?"

"I hope to, at least part of the year."

Unsure how she felt about his answer, she lifted her glass and tossed the rest of the wine right down her throat. It was like throwing gasoline on a fire. She choked, gasped for air, then went through a series of coughing and sputtering.

Max jumped up, slapped her on the back, then got her a glass of water.

"You okay?" he asked.

Katie drank the water, then nodded. Everything had been going so well. She'd felt, well, so elegant having a fancy meal on a fancy boat. Then she had to go and ruin it by choking on her wine.

As they drove away from the boat dock, Katie rubbed her hand across her burning throat and sipped on the bottle of water Max had provided.

"I need to make a quick stop before we go back, if that's all right?" The question was moot as he didn't wait for her reply but took the road leading away from town. Soon they were driving up to The Bayside Inn.

"I hope you don't expect me to go in there with you." She looked askance at her clothing.

"Don't worry, I have a private entrance." With that, he proceeded to the back of the beautiful rambling white inn. Moments later, Max unlocked a dark green door made of thick beveled glass and wood. They entered a wide hallway, which led to a set of elevator doors at the opposite end.

In seconds, the elevator opened onto the foyer of the fourth-floor suite. She walked slowly through the apartment, taking in the magnificent surroundings. Beautiful antique furniture, polished to a warm patina, was interspersed with sleek modern, upholstered pieces comfortably spaced throughout the large room. Everything was open and airy, the placement of the furniture acting as room dividers. Captivated, Katie walked over to the large paned-glass windows and French doors that opened onto a large balcony. She looked out over the hotel's private marina on which hung strand upon strand of soft white lights that seemed to dance pirouettes over the moonlit water.

"It's beautiful, Max," she said in a soft voice. "You have everything."

"Not everything, Katie."

He paused, then opened his mouth as if to say something else, when his phone rang, spoiling the moment with its shrill demand to be answered.

With a heavy sigh, Max lifted the receiver.

"Yes," he snapped, obviously aggravated with the interruption.

"Markesan wants what? You're here now?" He glanced quickly at his watch. "Oh, all right, come on up." Max hung up the phone and met her gaze, regret apparent in his brown eyes. "Katie, I'm sorry. Do you mind seeing yourself home?"

Her eyes held his as she shook her head. He held out the Jeep keys. As she reached out to take them, his warm strong fingers wrapped around hers and held tightly. The contact caused a strange and wonderful tug on her heart.

"Come on, I'll walk you down."

Without releasing her hand, Max saw her to her vehicle.

Her body still warm from his touch, Katie checked the beveled glass door in her rearview mirror. Her heart sank to her feet.

Max was re-entering his apartment, while laying a casual arm across the back of Sal's shoulders.

## Chapter 14

Tuesday was rainy and cold. Max and Pop sat comfortably in front of the fire, pouring over some recently found records. Katie wished she would have been included but decided to spend the morning going through some boxes she'd brought over from her aunt's house. Curling up in bed, she tucked her jean-clad legs underneath her hips. She spent well over an hour going through each box, sifting through the assortment of paraphernalia and sorting the items into stacks.

"You've been mighty quiet up here. Max and I were wondering where you'd gotten to." Angus reached out with both hands and steadied his tall frame against the doorjamb.

"How's the research coming?"

"Mighty exciting. I never thought delving into one's family history could be so enlightening," Pop answered. "How about some hot chocolate?"

Katie stretched her arms over her head. "I'd love a cup, thanks. I just have one more box to go through. I've been putting this off long enough, and I'm determined to finish before I leave this room."

"All right, darlin'. Back in a jiffy."

"Be careful of those stairs," she hollered at his departing figure.

Katie finished stacking the "to keep" items, then dragged over the last box. She ripped the tape from the side of the box, gave it a slight turn, then yanked the rest of the tape off in one final jerk. She opened the flaps in front of her to reveal two stacks of letters bundled together with rubber bands. Katie slowly picked up a stack. Suddenly breathless and with fingers that shook, she removed the rubber band and watched as it broke into pieces. Staring up at her was the unmistakable bold script of her sailor. Stunned, she sat for a moment before her eyes fell on the stack of pink-bound envelopes still nestled inside. She felt the blood drain from her face. A sick feeling flooded her as she was hit with the awful truth of what her aunt had done.

She heard footsteps and glanced toward the doorway. Max was holding two cups of what looked like hot chocolate.

"Get out!" She cursed her sharp tone. How could Aunt Margaret have done this to her?

Max ignored her and stepped cautiously forward to place the hot liquid on the nearby chest.

"What's wrong?" he asked as he walked over to the bed, then picked up one of the letters.

"No, don't." Katie snatched the letter from Max's hand and shoved it along with the others back in the box. Max's gaze followed her actions and he stood staring at the box, as if transfixed.

Stricken, Katie ran from the room, startling Angus as she fled past him at the bottom of the stairs. In minutes, she was sprinting breathless through the icy rainfall then up the spiral steps of the lighthouse until she burst through the door onto the observation deck.

Katie stood shivering, her hands gripping the rail, her head slightly bent against the stinging rain. The door slammed behind her, and she cast her eyes in his direction. Of course, Max would be wearing warm rain gear.

"Come out of the rain, Katie. You'll catch your death."

"That hasn't bothered you before," she said, her voice raspy from crying.

"Angus is worried about you." When she didn't say anything, he continued. "I don't know what's got you so upset, but you need to come inside."

"You don't understand. My aunt . . ." She swallowed hard, forcing herself to continue. "She, she withheld some letters. Letters that mean a lot to me."

"Look, your aunt is pure poison, as far as I'm concerned. But don't you think you're being just a bit melodramatic?"

"I don't need any commentary from you. You don't understand. And you never will."

"I know you don't, but you're going to get my opinion just the same."

Katie spun to face him, her hair plastered over her head, the pelting rain stinging her eyes. "You know nothing about it."

"Tell me."

From Max's determined expression, Katie knew he wouldn't stop until he heard the truth. She took a deep breath, then told him everything, except for the kiss. That was too dear to her heart to share with someone as bossy as Max. He'd never understand.

When she'd finished, he said, "I know you won't believe me, Katie, but you've built this guy up into some perfect paragon that no real man could compete with. Sure, you were given a bum deal, but how many more years of your life are you going to give over to this phantom of yours?"

"He's not a phantom. I have his letters to prove it."

"Oh, he may be real enough, but believe me, he's nothing like the picture you've painted of him."

"You have no idea, Max." She turned her back to him and stared out at the tumultuous sea. "You only see black and white. You can't imagine what it's like to be in love."

The wind and rain had picked up, and Katie had to strain to hear his reply. "You know what I think? I think you like living in the past. In fact, you're so wrapped up in it that you can't even recognize the life that's right in front of you. You'd rather think yourself in love with a phantom. You'd rather spend your life doting on an old man who would much rather be free to get on with his own life, however long that might be."

Katie turned to face him, anger churning low in her gut.

"You're in love with bricks and mortar, Katie McCullough, with a twenty-four-year-old who no longer exists, with a memory, for God's sake." His eyes raked over her. "You'd rather go out on a date with a nine-year-old boy. How utterly safe for you."

Enraged, Katie raised her right hand and slapped Max across the face.

But Max didn't miss a beat. "You wouldn't know what to do with a real man if he was staring you in the face." Through the pelting rain, his mocking eyes challenged her. And before Katie could respond, Max pulled her hard against his chest and covered her lips with the rough pressure of his own. She pushed hard against him, arching her back away as she did so. But Max's powerful arms and firm lips continued with a pressure both frightening and compelling in its intensity and had her clinging desperately to him for support. Suddenly, she was returning his kisses with a fervor she didn't know she possessed. Just as suddenly, Max released her, leaving her breathless and wanting more.

"Let's see how that holds up to bricks and mortar." He took hold of her arm, pulling her out of the rain and toward the staircase.

"I'm not going anywhere with you," she spat out, jerking herself from his hold.

"I'm not returning without you." He strengthened his grip, rendering her impotent in any and all attempts to pull free from his hold.

"You are the most hateful man." Despite her words, she had no choice but to follow him down the stairs.

It stormed most of the night, but by Wednesday morning the sun was peeking through the last of the dark clouds. Max, about to pass by Katie's bedroom door, stopped when he saw her curled up in her chair, the stack of unopened letters now sitting on her desk. For a moment, he watched her as she sat with her chin in her hand, her ponytail revealing the vulnerable nape of her neck. He clenched his jaw as anger toward her aunt flared in his gut, but he wasn't about to let Katie sit around in self-pity because of it.

"Well, are you going to read them?"

Katie's head came up sharply, and he caught a glimpse of her red-rimmed eyes before she turned her back to him. "Go away."

He stepped inside her room and asked, "Afraid?" He shook his head. "Poor Katie, afraid to live in the present and afraid to go forward. No wonder the past is so appealing to you."

He deliberately baited her, hoping to shake her out of her despondency. He hated seeing her like this. To be honest, he missed her impish smile. Missed her sparring, and her sass. He missed her.

"I'm sorry I hit you," she whispered.

Something inside him released as he studied Katie's pinched and drawn face. He stuffed his hands deep within his pockets. "I'm sure I deserved it," he stated flatly, then turned and went down the stairs.

Friday night, Bessie came to pick up Pop for a Christmas concert at church, but Katie complained of a headache and stayed behind. Before he left, Pop had built Katie a fire and lovingly tucked an afghan around her legs, which she'd propped on the plaid ottoman.

"It's a mean, evil, thing she's done to you to be sure,' he

mumbled as he tucked her in.

"Thank you," Katie said, and meant it. Pop had been so sweet. He could tell she'd been terribly upset, so in his own way he'd tried to take care of her.

Max had gone out tonight as well, probably with Sal. Katie laid her head back against the old chair and closed her eyes. She sat like this for a few minutes, giving the pain medication time to work its wonders. Soon the fire crackled in the distance, and sound faded away as the warmth from the flames lulled her to sleep.

She awoke some time later and noticed that the fire was dancing brightly in its grate. Obviously, someone had put more logs on it. She sat up and looked around, and her gaze fell on the box of letters sitting on the coffee table. She reached over to pick them up and as she did so a piece of paper fell to the floor. She picked it up and read. *Don't give way to fear, angel. It is a thief that will rob you of your life.*

Katie spent the next hour reading her sailor's letters. She smiled when she opened the first letter and read his familiar greeting. *Keeper girl*. It was the name he'd given her, what he always called her. She transported back in time to when she was eighteen. According to the date of the letter, that's how old she would have been. He'd signed it the way he'd signed all of his letters to her, *Your Sailor*.

Katie got up and fixed herself a scone and some hot green tea. Glancing out the window, she smiled as she watched their first snowfall of the season. Curling back up in front of the fire, she opened the next letter. As she read, Katie was filled with a sweet, poignant longing. Through his writing, he had revealed a sort of claim over her that wasn't at all unappealing.

A short while later, she roused herself to stoke the logs and turned as Pop and Max entered the cottage, smiling a welcome as they shook the snow of their coats.

"How was the Christmas concert? Where's Bessie?" She scanned the area behind them.

"Max brought me home so Bessie wouldn't have to. And the concert was very nice. We all missed you, darlin'," Pop replied. "Are you feeling better?"

She nodded. "Someone came in and put more logs on the fire while I was asleep, either that or logs multiply while they're burning nowadays," she said, unable to keep her eyes from straying in Max's direction.

A smile creased his handsome face. "As quiet as I was adding logs to the fire, there was that one moment when you stirred in your sleep. Buddy's tail thumped so hard at my appearance." Max continued to regard her with amusement, then added, "Angus called to let me know that you wouldn't be joining us, so I thought I'd stop by and check on you before I met them there."

"Making sure I had a headache, more like." She teased him with a smile, breathless at the thought that he'd checked on her. Maybe there was hope for him, after all.


Unable to sleep that night as a result of her long nap earlier that evening, Katie decided to slip out to her aunt's house to work on her sixth painting. This last one was the Light at St. Simons Island, Georgia. With each stroke of her brush, Katie wondered if Sally Batson was ever going to call.

In the wee hours of the morning, after setting her alarm for work, she crawled underneath her quilt, but sleep evaded as her thoughts ran rampant in regards to her sailor and Max. How could two very different men have captured her heart? One sweet and tender; the other high-handed and aggravating. She could not deny the internal battle waging within, as her heart seemed to betray the one while it longed for the other. Why was it so hard to let her sailor go? Was she really foolish enough to think that he would show up after all these years? Questions bombarded her as she tried to fall asleep. Could the real man even compete with the memory? Jill had scoffed that no one could, but Katie knew otherwise.

## Chapter 15

Sunday night the tree-trimming party was in full swing when Buddy's tail enthusiastically swatted the evergreen boughs, knocking off his third ornament for the evening. Katie swept the sparkly glass pieces into the dustpan, then threw them away before assisting Bessie and Lily with the buffet dinner. The table was already laden with oysters on the half shell, crab cakes, small hot biscuits and ham, carrot soufflé, a hot curried fruit compote, as well as an assortment of chips, crackers, and dipping sauces.

Max entered with Nate and one of his youngest brothers, Seth, but otherwise dateless. She breathed a sigh of relief. That removed a level of awkwardness from the evening.

He carried a tray of tiny Christmas cakes, beautifully decorated by the chef at The Bayside Inn. "Compliments of Sean Day," he said gaily as he lowered the tray onto the tall chest in the parlor that had been cleared off to serve the desserts. Max followed with introductions as Nate and Seth entered close behind, carrying an assortment of pies.

Lily called everyone into the small kitchen, and Angus asked the blessing, then they all lined up around the table to fill their decorative Christmas plates. The little cottage filled with laughter and joy and the best seasonal fare the Chesapeake Bay had to offer.

Katie went through the line last. She noticed Jill and Seth sitting close together on the sofa. She smiled as she watched her friend sparkle. She'd never seen Jill light up like that with anyone before.

She settled herself on the floor beside Jamey, who was

busy stringing the last of the popcorn. She took note of the major discrepancy between the popcorn left in the bowl and the amount of string that had yet to be strung, and couldn't resist asking, "Jamey, what happened to all the popcorn?" He looked up at her, his greasy kernel corn lips breaking into a sheepish grin.

"Oh, no, here comes your sister. Wipe your mouth," she whispered with mock urgency while he quickly wiped the evidence off with the back of his sleeve.

Jill joined them on the floor at the foot of the Christmas tree. "I thought I'd help before all of the popcorn goes missing," she said pointedly to her little brother, then grinned at his startled expression.

Katie laughed, set her empty plate on the floor beside her, and leaned back on her hands to scan the room. Nate and Seth had gotten up and were poring over the dessert bar as if it were the most important decision of their lives. Lily was making her way to the desserts as well, and Bessie and Pop were still eating their dinner. Tom and Max were deep in discussion. Both leaned toward the other, their arms resting on their thighs. Each held a tumbler in his hands, which looked suspiciously like something other than fruit punch. She wondered what could have them both so riveted. Max had that thoughtful frown she'd come to recognize as boding ill for someone. Tom seemed to be doing most of the talking, and Max the listening, which was highly unusual for him. Suddenly, he turned toward her, catching her off guard. Their eyes locked, and he looked at her with a peculiar smoldering expression.

*Uh, oh.* Katie looked away first, then grabbed her empty plate. She scurried to her feet right as Seth was walking by with a small plate of assorted sweets for her to try. Although he was holding out the plate to her, his gaze was locked on Jill. Katie looked from Seth to Jill and noticed that she, too, was staring right back at him with a sweet expression. Katie smiled, plucked a yummy looking confection off the plate, then went to the kitchen to start the clean up.

Katie smiled outright as she placed the plate in the sink, then turned on the tap. Neither one had noticed her departure.

"You look like the proverbial cat that swallowed the canary," Max said as he entered the kitchen with a tray of dirty dishes, which he set on the counter beside her.

Katie's lips curled as she looked up at him. "Don't tell me you haven't noticed. Or, maybe not."

"What is that supposed to mean?" Max unloaded the dishes off the tray.

"You and Tom sure had your heads together most of the evening, so how could you notice anything else going on right under your nose? Frankly, you looked ready to strangle somebody. What were you two talking about?" Katie asked while she scrubbed one of the plates.

"Nothing you need to worry yourself with."

"So what happened to your date?" She inwardly cringed at the question.

"What date?"

"The one you said you were going to bring to the party. Remember? When we talked about who would be coming?" Katie turned and looked him square in the face.

Max gave her a slight smile and smoothed the area between her brows with his thumb. "You'll get frown lines if you keep doing that."

Katie yanked her head back, feeling her frown deepening as she did so.

"I don't recall saying I would bring a date. I did bring Nate and Seth, though. Don't they count?"

Exasperated, Katie shook her head, and turned back to the sink.

"So what happened right under my nose, angel?"

"Seth and Jill, that's what."

He smiled as he picked up a tea towel and started to

wipe the plate she handed him. "Is that such a bad thing?"

"That all depends. Is he the 'love 'em and leave 'em' type?" Her soapy hands delved back into the hot, sudsy water. "Jill has a sensitive heart."

"Hmm, let me think. To date, Seth hasn't been serious about anyone that I know of, but I can tell you that he is a young man of moral character, upstanding in his community, and I believe has a bright future in the business world."

"Sounds like a remarkable catch. Maybe I should bat my eyes in his direction." She turned toward Max and proceeded to flutter her lashes coyly up at him.

Before she knew it, Max wrapped his arms around her and clasped her firmly to him. Caught completely off guard, she gazed up at him. With her lips softly parted, she waited with bated breath for the kiss she knew was coming. Max lowered his head a fraction and instead of kissing her, he stared at her, searching her with eyes that devoured. Katie closed her eyes.

"Hey, I know what you guys are doing."

Embarrassed, Katie's eyes flew open. Color rushed her cheeks. Of all people, Jamey had to be the one who found them like this. She pushed at Max's chest, and to her frustration, he continued to hold her. "Let go," she said between clenched teeth.

"Oh, and just what is you caught us doing?" Max asked, grinning down at Jamey.

"What Mom and Dad do when they don't think I'm looking." He grinned up at them.

"Then I suggest you run along so we can finish before anyone else decides to help with the dishes."

"We? I had nothing to do with this," she said.

"You bat your eyes like that at me again, and believe me, I won't be held accountable for my actions."

"Let me go right this instant," Katie snapped. "He will tell everybody out there."

He let her go so abruptly that she nearly fell backward. He reached out to steady her as Lily walked in.

"Hey, you've been working in here long enough. I'll take over for now. You two go on out and visit."

Katie held a pillow across her chest as she lay in bed later that night. Everyone had had such a great time, especially Pop. He had laughed and told lighthouse stories most of the evening to anyone who would listen. She had never seen him look happier. She grudgingly admitted that she had Max to thank for that. He had accomplished in six weeks what she hadn't been able to do in years. Thinking of Max, she frowned as she remembered the conspiratorial wink that had passed between him and Jamey as everyone departed for the evening. Even Jamey was in cahoots with him. She hugged the pillow closer to her chest. She recalled the war she had waged against him not long after they met and realized she was imminently close to losing it. Except for the first few skirmishes, she'd lost every battle in between.

As she fell asleep, her thoughts lingered over the moment in the kitchen when Max held her, his gaze devouring every inch of her face. She loved his golden brown eyes and sleepily admitted they could feast on her anytime they wanted.

## Chapter 16

The painters arrived at eight the following Monday morning to finish up the trim work. With a strong cup of coffee in hand, Katie walked over to the main house shortly after their arrival to greet them and to see if they needed anything. Max and Angus were in town having their weekly breakfast at Phil's, something he had started the week they had moved in. At first, she had felt left out, but then realized that Pop had needed male companionship and that having it come from a younger man who had similar interests was like a healing balm to his frail, arthritic limbs. Even Bessie with all her tender care hadn't been able to do that for him.

Katie walked over to the light and trudged up the tower steps. She entered the lantern room and trailed her gloved hand carefully over the thick glass of the lens before stepping outside. As she leaned into the rail, her warm breath hit the cold air and rose like hot steam from coffee. Inhaling deeply, she closed her eyes and listened at the sound of the bell buoy thumping out its occasional ding as it bobbed in the bay. Opening her eyes, she watched a lone seagull soaring nearby, content just to be free. Since the sun was behind the lighthouse, Katie enjoyed the tower's shadow lying quietly on the ground below, always amazed at the perfect shape that splayed across the ground.

"Katie." At the familiar voice of her warden, Katie turned toward Max. "Angus wasn't feeling too well so we came back early." She must have appeared concerned because he added, "Probably too much excitement last night, but ..."

"I'd better check on him." She brushed past him and quickly left the platform.

Katie entered the parlor, and she immediately noticed Pop's ashen face. She hurried to the sofa where he lay propped up with some pillows.

"I'm all right, Katie. I'm just needin' to catch my breath," he said as he lightly patted her arm.

"Are you sure? You don't look so good. Should I call Doc Stevens?"

"Ach, no! I won't be needin' a doctor."

His speech pattern raised her level of concern. Pop only resorted to his thick Irish drawl whenever he was really fretful, which was seldom, if ever, but a sure sign he wasn't too happy with his current condition.

"What about Bessie?"

"Don't ya be worry'n her, either. I tell ya, I just need ta catch me breath. Now run along. You're becoming tiresome, girl."

Katie rose from the cushion and felt her brows furrow as she made her way toward Max. "Except for once when he was exasperated with my aunt, I've never in my whole life seen him like this."

"Hmm, cantankerous. Maybe you two *are* related." Max gazed at her with amusement, but the smile didn't quite reach his eyes. "Fix him some tea, while I make a phone call," he said as he strode from the room.

Twenty minutes later, while Katie and Angus sipped their tea, Max came in with Doc Stevens.

"Katie, I thought I told you, no doctor." Pop's face darkened and his voice rose.

"She didn't call him. I did," Max said with that air of authority Katie thought he only used with her.

"Calm down, Angus. You know you're only hurting yourself with such stubbornness," the doctor said. The tall wiry man in his mid fifties smiled at Pop, then leaned down to check his patient's pulse. "Are you taking your meds?"

Angus grunted. "I told you before, Doc. I don't believe in pills. Lived my whole life without them."

"Well, that won't be for much longer if you don't start taking them," Doc admonished, but with a kindness and attentiveness Katie admired. She wished she had half the patience he demonstrated as he worked on Pop.

A short while later on the front porch, Doc Stevens patted her on the shoulder and told her not to worry. Easier said than done. Sleep would not come easy tonight. She'd lost everyone else in her life. She couldn't lose Pop.

The next afternoon as he left his study, Max passed by Katie's door and saw her curled up in her chair with a pensive expression on her face, the letters which she had placed in a pretty decorative box on her lap. At the light tap on her door, she turned toward him.

"I would offer a penny for them, but I'm sure they're more expensive than that," he said.

She smiled in return. "Truthfully, I've been trying to figure out how my letter got to him in the first place." She sat fingering the ribbon that tied the lid to the box.

Max moved forward into the room as she spoke. At the ring of his phone, he glanced at the display before stuffing it and his hands into his pants pockets.

"Mrs. G. I'll call her back later."

"Oh yeah, she knows your mother, doesn't she?"

"She does. I'm having dinner with her tonight."

"You know she's the person who's responsible for all of this," she said, holding up the box.

"Is that right?"

"Yeah, she was my ninth grade English teacher and she started this Letters to Troops program."

As Katie continued, Max perched his large frame on

the edge of her bed.

"How my class got his unit is beyond me. There must have been some sort of connection." Katie shook her head as she curled up at the foot of her bed. Max watched her as she suddenly became more animated, her eyes taking on a delicate sparkle.

"When he answered my first letter, I knew he was my lighthouse sailor because he called me by the name he had given me that night. Isn't that amazing?"

"I can only imagine." Max watched her glowing response to his smile of understanding. Katie moved up to her knees, then sat her rear end back down on her heels.

"There was a wonderful mystery about him," she continued with wistful poignancy.

Max's jaw tightened as he watched her lovely eyes take on a misty longing. "So what did he look like?"

Katie's smile turned sheepish. "I ... don't know."

Max raised a brow in her direction.

"Well it was dark and he was in shadow ... so I really couldn't ... see him very well," she ended lamely. "And before you even ask, no, I don't have a picture of him. He wouldn't send me one. That I have yet to figure out," she muttered under her breath. Sighing heavily, Katie stared down at her quilt, lightly fingering one of its patterns. "There was something about him," she said softly. "Maybe it was because he was such a mystery that I found myself telling him things that I'd never told anybody else."

"What things?" he asked quietly, although he already knew the answer.

Katie lifted her eyes to his, the blue almonds taking on a depth of longing. "Every desire of my heart." In one movement, Katie hugged her knees to her chest.

Max drank in her slender curves, draped in a sweater, her long fingers delicately displaying a ring on each hand.

"I was so sad when he stopped writing. I just didn't

understand what I had done."

Max clenched his jaw and felt his gut lurch as he watched Katie's eyes cloud over.

She slid off the bed, then proceeded to rub her palms back and forth over her thighs.

Riveted, Max watched as several emotions crossed Katie's face before she clearly came to some revelation that seemed to jerk her out of her reverie.

"So let me get this straight, you write this guy for two years, you don't know his name, and you have no clue what he looks like."

The sparkle in her blue eyes faded to smoldering chips of annoyance. "You would see it that way. I thought I could talk to you."

"Well, someone needs to ground you in reality." The sudden shrill of the cell phone interrupted her. "Mrs. G again. I need to take this," he stated and strode from the room.

Over the next week, Katie observed Pop become a different person. He had decided to take his medications, and the results to his physical well-being were remarkable.

Thoughts of her future loomed up, worrying her more and more. Her time of work was nearing an end. And the thought of moving to her aunt's house or to the attic room again frankly depressed her. She still hadn't heard from Miss Batson, either, and even if she could just sell her paintings outright, that, too, would take time and the right contacts.

A few days later on Christmas Eve, Paige Point awoke to a blanket of snow. But the salt trucks had been out since the early hours of the morning and already had most of the roads clear. While scrambling eggs, she noticed the foreman's truck drive off the property and wondered what he and the crew were doing here at this early hour, in this weather, and on Christmas Eve of all days. She shrugged as she retrieved the toast when it popped up. Bessie arrived shortly after eleven o'clock and picked up Pop for Christmas Eve festivities at the retirement home. Katie had to smile at the spring in his step as Pop accompanied Bessie to her car.

Katie donned her warm jacket and made the ten-minute drive to Jill's apartment.

She sprinted up the steps to the second floor of what used to be an old boarding house. Jill's suite of rooms was a blend of art deco finds and colorful modern pieces, a look not unlike Jill's very own wardrobe.

Katie plopped down at the kitchen table while Jill ladled up oyster stew.

"What's that? My Christmas gift?" Jill asked when she spotted the container.

"Nope." Katie shoved the box across the table toward her friend. "Open it."

Jill eyed Katie, clearly intrigued. Untying the ribbon, she lifted the lid while Katie took a sip of her tea.

"So you brought me letters from your sailor?"

"Look at the dates."

Jill picked up the letters and flipped through them, reading the postmarks as she did so. "I thought he stopped writing you two and a half, three years ago," Jill said, brow furrowed.

Katie slowly explained what her aunt had done and Max's insistence that she read them. "He feels I'm wasting my life for a phantom."

Jill stared at her with a look that spoke volumes, but all she said was, "How awful for you."

"It was, actually, and the really awful thing is that he'll never know what happened."

"Let's read the letters and look for clues. Maybe we can figure out where he is?"

"I've thought about it so much lately that I'm batty. You look for clues. This whole thing has me exhausted." Katie slipped out of her chair and walked over to the seamstress mannequin to finish attaching the cluster of curling fabric onto the bodice. "Are you sure about this ruffle?"

"I'm telling you they're in right now." Then, after a pause, she continued. "You don't seem very interested in him."

"I'm interested, of course I'm interested. It's just that I'm confused." She pulled a straight pin from the pincushion and slid it through the fabric. "I'm just trying to figure it all out."

"What's there to figure out? Phantom letter guy, or devastatingly attractive male right under your roof guy?"

"I wish it were that simple."

Katie was driving back to the cottage when her cell rang from somewhere deep inside her purse. "Darn." The Jeep swerved as she immediately dug for her phone. She immediately thought of Davy and sobered. With great care and without taking her eyes off the road, she felt in her bag until she found her phone.

"Katie, thank goodness you answered," Bessie's shrill voice said. "It's Angus, dear, he's in the hospital."

# Chapter 17

Tired to her bones, Katie arrived back at the cottage, let Buddy inside, then stooped to plug in the tree lights. After fixing a mug of hot chocolate, she turned on the radio, collapsed into the chair, and tried to relax while she listened to the carols. Pop was stable. For now. He'd suffered a mild heart attack.

As she sipped on the sweet confection, she glanced at the small array of packages under the tree. Although there were only a few, each was beautifully wrapped with glittery red paper and silver bows. Something for everyone on her list. She had struggled with what to get Max, and after much mental debate, his small gift was tucked under the tree as well.

On impulse, Katie walked over to the tree and sat down, crossing her legs beneath her. As she gazed at the beautiful tree, a smile lit up her features. After a moment's hesitation, she lay down on her back and scooted her body under the low boughs. For the longest time, she gazed up into the most amazing enchanted glass and tinsel forest. Closing her eyes, she breathed deeply, inhaling the fragrant evergreen branches. As she did so, the song "All is Well" started playing on the radio. The words began to flow over her, bringing comfort and a much-needed sleep.

When she opened her eyes some time later, she found a pair of tawny brown eyes staring right at her. Max was on the floor lying on his side, propped up on one elbow, with Buddy sprawled out nearby. A slow smile spread across his features at her reaction to his presence. Chagrined, Katie started edging her way out from under the tree.

"Don't move on my account. I rather like you under there. Are you someone's Christmas present?" He was clearly amused.

Katie pulled a face. "No, I am not someone's Christmas present."

"Pity," he drawled. "So what are you doing under there?"

"I was losing myself in a world of fantasy. Would you like to try it?"

"I thought you'd never ask." He slid his massive form underneath. Katie moved to slip out from under the tree, but Max grabbed hold of her arm to halt her retreat. She looked down at him and thought how wonderfully gorgeous he was. His eyes smiled at her as he tugged her back down next to him. He stared up through the branches and asked, "What do you see?"

Katie tore her eyes away from his profile and looked up. "I see joy, anticipation, magic ..." She turned toward him and was unprepared for the look he was giving her. She ran her tongue over suddenly dry lips and asked, "What do you see?"

His look deepened, holding her spellbound. "I see you." He drew her to him, and placed his lips against hers. It was a sweet, lingering kiss that warmed her entire being. Max lifted his head, then ran his thumb across her mouth.

Katie searched his face. "Why are you here?" she whispered. "Why did you come back?"

Max stroked her hair away from her face. "Bessie called me about Angus. I came back as soon as I could. I've already been to the hospital."

"Oh." A slight wave of disappointment washed over her, and shamefully she pushed it away.

"Angus is going to be all right, Katie."

Katie smiled tremulously and nodded her head. Max

helped her up off the floor and proceeded to start a fire. "Are you hungry?" he asked, glancing at her over his shoulder.

"Yes, I'll throw something together, but don't expect anything fancy." She turned toward the kitchen. "Pop and I were supposed to have dinner with Bessie in her apartment at the retirement home."

"Look in the refrigerator."

Perplexed, Katie walked into the kitchen and opened the fridge door. It was filled with platters of food. Katie pealed back the foil covering to reveal tenderloin, green beans almandine, potato salad, baked chicken, grilled salmon, and several cold pasta salads. On the bottom shelf sat an incredible-looking three-tiered coconut cake.

"Find anything you like in there?" he called from the parlor.

"Did you bring all of this with you?" she called.

"After I saw Angus, I phoned ahead and alerted Sean and left it in his capable hands. He met me halfway and we loaded the trunk of my car."

"But there's enough in there for a week."

"Good, enjoy it." He rose from stoking the fire and grinned at her standing there with mouth gaping. "So are you going to heat something up, or do I have to do everything around here?"

Katie returned his grin and flitted back into the kitchen.

She and Max sat together in front of the fire and enjoyed a meal on her blue willow dishes, sipping wine from her mother's crystal. She didn't mind anymore about her possessions. None of them loomed in importance as they once had. Curling up on the sofa, Katie tucked her feet underneath her as Max poured her another glass of wine. She normally didn't drink, so she was unprepared for the light-headedness she was feeling. She laid her head back against the sofa and closed her eyes.

"Have you finished the letters?"

Katie slowly opened her eyes and faced Max, who sat twirling his wine glass between long fingers, legs outstretched in front of him.

"Yes, I've finished them."

"And ...?"

"He was coming to see me, said he had something to tell me," she said as she looked back down at her glass. "I'm sure my aunt took care of him on his visit. Another thing I can thank her for," she added bitterly.

"I've never known you to give in to self pity, Katie."

She looked over at him somewhat startled by his words. Max returned her look with an expression on his handsome face that was hard to read.

"Well, you haven't known me very long," she said, her eyes suddenly filling with unshed tears.

Max looked at her for a long moment, then asked, "How do you know he came?"

"I just know. He wouldn't lie."

"It's a lucky man that has your trust, Katie McCullough."

Katie's eyes were riveted on Max as he spoke, surprised at what she was hearing.

"Have you ever tried to find him?" He leaned forward and stared down at his empty glass as he placed it on the small table at his feet.

"I wrote him a letter in October. I came across his address and even though it was several years old, I thought, what the heck, I'll try one more time." She gave Max a somewhat brave but cynical little smile. "Jill says he's probably married with a couple of kids by now." Katie shrugged and tossed the rest of the wine straight down her throat, which had her coughing and grimacing. Max rose from the sofa and took the glass from Katie's unresisting fingers. "I think you've had enough."

"Don't tell me when I've had enough," she snapped, irritated by his bossiness.

Max held out his hand. Suddenly, tired of fighting with him, she placed her hand in the strength of his. His warm clasp made her feel safe and secure. Sighing, she rose to her feet, walked with him to the door, then watched as he wrapped the navy scarf around his neck. "I'm driving back tonight. I wish you'd come home with me. My mother would love it. She's outnumbered, you know." He gave her one of his teasing smiles she'd secretly come to love.

"It's tempting, but I wouldn't feel right spending Christmas away from Pop."

"I understand. Now, grab your coat and walk me to my car. I want to give you your Christmas present."

Katie hesitated, surprise written all over her face. "Oh, I have your present, too." She hurried back into the parlor to grab Max's gift, then shyly handed him his present. "I meant to give it to you before you left. Merry Christmas, Max."

"Thank you, Katie." His smile as he took her gift seemed genuine, not his usual teasing or mocking one.

"Should I open it now?"

"Of course." She all but bobbed up on her toes like an excited child. She caught the amused light in his eyes and stilled her feet. She flushed with embarrassment, feeling like a silly schoolgirl. Max's long fingers untied the bow and tore the sparkly red paper away from the gift. She held her breath as she waited for his reaction. His grin faded as his mouth dropped open.

"Katie, this is wonderful." It was a pen and ink drawing of the light station as it had been in the days when the buildings were on site with the tower. She'd worked hard on the composition, intending to be not only accurate, but pleasing to the eye.

"I mean it, this is very good. Who's the artist?"

Inordinately pleased with his critique of her work, she answered shyly, "Me."

Max's gaze flew to hers. "Katie, I had no idea you

could draw like this. I was under the impression that your art interest was interior design." He studied the drawing. "Where's your signature?"

She chuckled. "It's there, just hard to see in this poor light. Oh, here," she said, reaching for a nearby pencil. She signed it to him in the bottom left-hand corner. *For Max, Merry Christmas, Katie.* "There, you can see that."

"I'll always treasure this, Katie. Thank you."

"I'm glad you like it."

"Now get your coat."

"Come on, Buddy," she hollered as she slid her arms into her jacket. Max opened the door, then put his hands over Katie's eyes and slowly walked her down the front steps.

"Watch it, careful," he instructed as she stepped gingerly down each step with his assistance.

"Max, what are you doing?" She laughed.

"Be patient, angel." Max lowered his hands away from her eyes. Standing before her was the most gaudy but glorious sight she had ever seen. Hundreds of multicolored Christmas lights streamed from the lighthouse. The cap, the rail, the candle room, as well as the entire body of the tower were covered in them. Katie's hands flew up to her face. "Oh, Max." She clasped her hands together. "It's beautiful. No one has ever done anything like this for me before. I ... I don't know what to say."

"Say yes."

"What?"

"To my asking you out on New Year's Eve."

She froze for a moment. He was asking her for a date. A real date. She opened her mouth to speak, then swallowed and said, "Yes." She looked up at him while the multi-colored glow surrounded them, which drew Katie's eyes back to the cascade of lights on the tower.

"How did you manage it?"

"My trusty foreman, of course. He put the lights on a

timer so they'll come on at dusk and go off around midnight. I'm glad you like it." Something in his voice had Katie turning back to him.

Max drew her into his arms and kissed her. His lips were warm against hers, fleeting as he lifted them to tease the sweet spot next to her mouth before claiming her lips again with a fervor that had her tingling all over. She was breathless when he released her. He wrapped his arms around her, hugging her close. "I have to go," he said, his voice husky. He held her from him and gave her a penetrating look that had her going weak at the knees. He placed a finger against her lips. "Hold my place."

Katie watched him drive away. She told Max she was going to hang outside so she could look at her lights, but it was really so she could see him until he was out of sight.

With a flashlight in hand, she mounted the spiral steps and approached the heart on the wall, and as was her custom, she slid down to sit near it, leaning her right shoulder against the wall.

"I think it's time," she said as a smile hovered on her lips. "I just want you to know, you paved the way." And for what she knew would be the last time she lifted her fingers to her lips and placed them against the heart in goodbye. Glowing with anticipation, Katie jumped up and ran down the stairs.

Later in bed, Katie gazed at the lighthouse. A slow smile parted her lips. She no longer loved a memory, but a man.

## Chapter 18

On Christmas day, Katie arrived at the hospital bearing gifts that she and Pop opened with smiles and hugs. Later, Bessie surprised them with a short visit around lunchtime laden with a dinner of traditional Christmas fare.

"Have you told her yet?" Bessie asked.

Katie looked expectantly toward Pop. "Told me what?"

A sheepish look sparkled from underneath gray bushy eyebrows followed by an even more sheepish grin. "Bessie and I are getting married. You don't mind, do you, Katie?"

Katie blinked at that. How could she have missed it? Was she that self-absorbed? That blind? Was she so afraid of being alone? So starved for love and affection that she happily boxed Pop up into her perfect plan with never a thought for what he might want?

"Oh, Pop, Bessie. Of course I don't mind, you sillies." Katie hugged them both and was completely floored when Angus excitedly added, "Max has offered us the cottage if we want it."

"Why that's ... wonderful," she said, her mind in a whirl. So Max knew they were getting married. As usual, Max seemed to know everything. With the discovery that Max and Pop were related, she really shouldn't be surprised. At least Pop's future was now settled. But what was to become of her?

The cleaning crew arrived two days after Christmas and attacked the finished construction site like fish on bait.

Katie heard the noise from the shop vacuum cleaners as she walked past the dormant rose bushes to check on the construction progress. She was surprised to see how much they had already accomplished, and two of the men had even started putting the furniture back in place so she assisted them for the remainder of the afternoon. Katie was pleased that Max had chosen to use her parents' furniture. Now a part of her would always belong here. He still didn't know that the furniture belonged to her, and she would never tell him. Besides, what was furniture when he already had her heart? For weeks, Katie had pondered the dramatic change in Max toward her, and as a result, a small hope soared in her heart that she, too, might have a place at the light station, but more importantly, with him.

Later, while dusting the upstairs office, her eyes fell on Davy's photo album. Unable to resist, she pulled the album off the shelf and sat down.

She smiled as she pored over the pages of photos, many of which were of her parents and her and Davy when they were little. Near the end of the album, she came to a photo that she had actually taken. It was of Davy and about five of his classmates at graduation. Her eyes went immediately to the broad smiling face of her brother. He was so handsome and so young, just a year older than she was now. She had been so proud of him, her big adorable brother. She remembered how he'd caught her eye and winked at her from the field below. She had grinned back from the stands, bursting with the joy of it all.

Katie closed the album and just as she lifted it to the shelf, a letter fell from its pages. She picked up the envelope, pausing when she noticed the familiar handwriting of her sailor. Before she could even contemplate why it was tucked in with her brother's album, she froze as she spotted the name across the top. Max, and it was addressed to Davy. Her fingers shook as she pulled the folded page from the envelope. With a pounding heart, Katie read the letter. It was brief, but revealed a firm friendship between the two with Max saying he looked forward to visiting Paige Point. Her breath caught in her throat. The date of his visit was the day Davy was killed.

Her body flashed cold, then hot. Oh God, it was Max. Max had been the one with Davy the day he was killed. Stunned, Katie opened the album to the group photo.

Her eyes roamed over the photograph and stopped to peer closely at one of the faces. Even though his cap was pulled low over his forehead, Katie was sure it was Max. She flipped the photo over. To her relief, her brother's handwriting had recorded the names of those on the other side. It took all of two seconds to find the name she was looking for.


On a cold, sunny morning, two days before the New Year, Katie and Jill drove into St. Michaels. They arrived, Katie with one of her watercolors and Jill with her two dresses in tow, for the afternoon fashion show. They entered the small but airy lobby of Falcon Designs, and Katie announced she was there to see Sally Batson.

"Heaven bless you. You came back." Sally gave Katie a brief hug, then chatted almost non-stop about how for the past several months they'd looked for her only to have a closed door at every turn.

"I am so sorry. I didn't realize ... didn't you get the note I left with my drawings? I had to leave, or I would have missed the last ferry."

"No, when I came back, the only things here were your sketches. And you are not leaving until I get every bit of your personal information." Sally laughed. "And we were just about to commit to using another artist's work, too. Your painting of Portland Head Light is breathtaking, Katie. If your other five paintings are half this brilliant, our client will be more than pleased, I can assure you. I'd like to keep this one to show my boss, if you don't mind."

"Of course," Katie replied, smiling broadly.

"Oh, what a beautiful ring," Jill exclaimed.

Sally, in the middle of writing down Katie's cell phone number, looked up at Jill and smiled. "Thank you. I think so, too." She raised her left hand to gaze down at the clear white diamond that sparkled on her finger. "Of course, the guy who goes along with it isn't half bad, either."

"You weren't engaged when I was here before, were you?" Katie asked politely.

"No, it just happened recently," she said as she continued writing, this time a check to Katie as a deposit for the art.

"Oh, you need to add my last name. It's McCullough," Katie said as she noticed Sally had only put her first two names on the check.

"I thought it was Clare?"

"No, that's my middle name. That's how I sign my work."

"Well, no wonder we couldn't find you ... Oh my gosh, you were the one who kept calling!" Color rushed high on Sally's cheeks.

"At least I know it's not personal." Relief swept through Katie. They liked her work. She had the job. Now all she had to do was talk to Max.


Later that evening, she and Jill sat down to dinner at The Bayside Inn at a table overlooking the bay. They'd had a wonderful day. Jill had come in second place and was very happy about it, especially after one of the judges asked for her contact information as he had an opening in his studio for someone with her fresh eye for color and design.

"Looks like you may have a real job before long," Katie said as she placed her napkin in her lap.

"I know. Can you believe it?" Jill replied as she took a sip of water. "You didn't do so badly today, either. Sally sure was taken with your painting."

"Thanks. I just hope her boss likes it as much as she does."

As Katie sipped on the hot, savory crab bisque, she thought how closely she had held her secret, that her sailor and Max were one in the same. She'd thought about it constantly since she'd found the letter. So many things now made sense—his arrival in the tower, his knowledge of things about her and Pop, and his connection to Mrs. G., and of course, to Davy. She sobered. He'd been there the day Davy had died. What exactly did Max know about what had happened to her brother?

Jill eyed Katie as she reached out for her iced tea. "Okay, something's up with you. That's the third time you've done that this evening."

"What?" She avoided Jill's perceptive gaze.

"You keep staring past my shoulder with this faraway look in your eyes."

Unable to contain it any longer, she blurted, "Max and my sailor are the same person." There. It was out. "But don't tell anybody," she quickly added. "Max doesn't even know that I know."

Jill's jaw dropped and her eyes slowly widened. "How in the world ...?" she began, then stopped as Katie filled her in.

"Katie, this is unbelievable. This is like Lois Lane finding out that Clark Kent is Superman."

Katie shook her head. "There's more." She swallowed hard. "I think Max was there the day Davy died."

"Oh, honey, I'm sorry." Jill clasped her hand and gave it a quick squeeze. "What are you going to do?"

She shook her head. "I don't know."

After several more minutes of conversation, Katie

followed Jill out the door of the restaurant into the clear, cold night. As they left the historic inn, Katie looked through a long window that opened onto a private dining room where a foursome seated in front of a roaring fire were in the act of raising their wine glasses in what looked to be a toast. The smile on Katie's lips faded as she recognized three of the four who sat there. Her heart plummeted to her stomach as she watched the familiar diamond-clad hand of Sally Batson wrap itself around the neck of Max Sawyer, pulling his head toward hers for a quick, laughing kiss. So Sally Batson and Sal were one and the same. Nate sat next to Sally, a huge boyish grin across his fine features. The older man sitting next to Max also watched with an indulgent expression on his face. The merry hearts in that intimate setting slapped Katie across the face with all the power of a gale force wind. Blinded by tears, she turned away, stumbling in her attempt to catch up with Jill.

*Well, what did you expect? What red-blooded male wouldn't freely accept any and all kisses from a pretty girl, especially one as willing as she?* Mortified, she shut her eyes as she thought of how she had responded to his kisses. Well one thing was for sure, she wouldn't be returning any of Max Sawyer's kisses ever again.

Hunkering down against the biting December wind, Katie scurried to the tower. Carrying the pail in one hand and a flashlight in the other, she took the spiral steps slowly, allowing her legs to thaw. Katie stopped at the spot and slid down to her knees.

"You were in front of me all this time and I didn't even recognize you," she whispered brokenly. With hands that shook, she dipped the brush into the white wash. In three strokes, the heart on the wall disappeared.

## Chapter 19

The next day, Pop was back home resting comfortably with an attentive Bessie by his side. They sat sipping hot cups of tea and discussing their upcoming wedding. Bessie quit her job at the retirement home and had moved into the cottage to take care of Pop during his recovery, thus allowing Katie to go forward with her plans to leave.

She slipped her arms into her jacket and trudged to the mailbox to send the check back to Sally Batson. So much had died with the return of that check. She could never afford to live in her aunt's house now, much less open her art gallery there. She could still hear Sally's voice when she'd called her that morning.

"Katie, I don't quite know how to tell you this, especially after our visit yesterday, but our firm has decided to use another artist for this project."

The rest of the conversation had been a blur. Stunned, Katie had tried to end the phone call as quickly as she could for fear she would burst into tears. As she wearily made her way back up to the house, she could still see Sally's lovely diamond-clad hand reaching around Max's neck with a haunting finality. Lovely and sophisticated Sally Batson. Katie could certainly see why Max would choose her.

New Year's Eve morning found Katie and Jill at the cottage, packing up her things.

"Hey, girl friend." Jill placed her arm around Katie's slumped shoulders. "Sherlock and Watson will be together.

It'll be fun, you'll see," Jill said in an effort to cheer her up.

Katie mustered a smile for Jill's benefit, but her heart was broken. Right now she just wanted to curl up in the fetal position. She would never be able to face Max again. She realized that if she now knew who he was, then he had to have known as well, and for a heck of a lot longer. Just the thought of him knowing completely mortified her. How she had *carried on* about her sailor's letters. It was too humiliating to even think about.

By noon, she was stoking the flames in the fireplace of the cabin and simmering some canned soup on the stove. After lunch, she and Buddy sauntered along the shoreline. Zombie-like, Katie stared into the distance, occasionally throwing a stick for Buddy to retrieve. Later, while curled up in front of the fire, she couldn't help but think about the last time she was here. As she gazed around the room, she could see Max's large, muscular frame everywhere—standing at the stove frying bacon, striding across the room, sleeping in the bottom bunk, his arms around her waist. Jumping up, she decided to take a walk. With flashlight in hand, she and Buddy crossed the few hundred yards to the water's edge. The stars shone bright and plentiful without the town lights to hide them. Not even Katie's shattered heart could alter their beauty. Her eyes turned toward the tower in the distance, faintly glowing with the colorful lights that she loved. Suddenly, the sky over Paige Point lit up with fireworks, bringing in the New Year. She stood there staring for a long time, then turned on the flashlight to mark her path back to the cabin.

Laying a couple more logs on the fire, Katie crawled into bed mentally exhausted, hoping sleep would stop the flow of memories. When she woke, her first thought was of Max. Max, Max, Max!

"I can't do this. I have to get out of here," she moaned.

The sooner she got to Jill's, the sooner she could get on with her life.

Buddy had already jumped inside the dingy when Katie reached the little boat. Climbing over the side, her gloved hand reached for the starter key. Her eyes grew wide as she saw it was missing, and she began to search for it.

"Missing something?"

Katie's head whipped around at the sound of Max's voice. He stood dangling the key in his right hand with a challenging expression on his face.

Katie sat speechless. Her heart lunged toward him, but her body stayed perfectly still. Her eyes devoured every inch of him. He was so handsome standing there in his dark gray cords, black jacket, and turtleneck sweater. Slowly, she climbed out of the boat and, still unable to trust her voice, walked toward him. Stopping just a few feet away, she held out her hand to receive the key.

But Max reared back like a pitcher on the mound and threw the key into the water. With mouth gaping, she watched the key fly through the air and splash into the water. She whipped around to face him. "What did you do that for?"

"Well, I'm glad to see you found your voice. I was actually getting concerned."

"How am I supposed to leave now?" she demanded, desperately wondering why he was standing there in front of her.

"I'll be happy to take you back after I eat. Boy, I'm hungry. Are you hungry?" He turned away and strode back toward the cabin. Katie opened her mouth to speak, but clamped it shut. She grabbed her backpack and stomped along after him.

Max was tossing logs on the grate when she entered. Katie slid out of her backpack, yanked off her gloves and jacket, and threw them on the bottom bunk. Max got down on his haunches to light the fire. Without looking at her, he said. "You stood me up last night."

The statement took Katie off guard. She licked dry lips. "Well what did you expect me to do under the circumstances?"

A slight frown formed on his handsome face. "I expected you to be dressed in your prettiest dress and ready for our date."

"And Sally ... what about her?" she asked, irritated he had the gall to confront her.

"Sally? What does she have to do with this?" Max drawled with maddening calm.

"What does she ...?" She paused, seeing red. "You know I've thought you were a lot of things, but not until recent events would I have thought you would cheat, two-time, the woman you're supposed to marry."

Max folded his arms across his chest and looked down at her with a disturbing gleam in his eyes. "Those are mighty strong words, angel. It's a good thing I'm in a magnanimous mood, or I'd make you back them up."

She opened her mouth to tell him just what she thought of him, but he beat her to the punch.

"Angus tells me you're leaving."

That brought her temper to a screeching halt and, somewhat flustered, she answered, "I ... yes, I am." She raised her chin a fraction. "Now that your research is done and the house is finished and now that Pop seems to be settled, I see no reason for me to stay. Jill is finishing up my packing and—"

"I told Jill to put a hold on it."

"What do you mean?"

"Packing you up and moving you out, that's what."

"You had no right to tell her that. I'll go wherever I darn well please, Max Sawyer. Your bossy days are over as far as I'm concerned."

"Fine, here's your key," he said, tossing it to her, completely unruffled by her outburst. The abruptness of his words caught her off guard. She looked up at him.

"That wasn't your key I threw in the water," he said.

Clutching the key against her chest, Katie stood there uncertain what she should do.

"Go on, get outta' here." Max towered over her, an unreadable expression on his face.

For a second, Katie's gaze locked with his. Then with a quick nod of her head, she hastily snatched up her coat and gloves, turned, and reached for the doorknob.

"Just one thing, though. Where would you like me to send your mother's silver?"

Katie stopped in her tracks.

She turned back toward him. Max stood leaning against the logs, hands stuffed in his pockets, his eyes holding hers in steady regard.

"As well as the other various and sundry items, like ... everything on the property," he said. "Although I suppose I could just offer to buy you out, but I'm sure that's not a very satisfying way to recoup two entire years of your life?"

"How ...?" Katie asked in a hoarse whisper.

Max pushed his shoulders away from the wall and walked toward her. Raising a hand up to his chin as if deep in thought, he said, "Or, maybe I could just offer you a partnership, but as I own the houses, I expect they cost a bit more than the furniture. So I might have to have something else to make things a little more even?"

A tear escaped from the corner of Katie's eye as she continued to stare up at him. Max stopped in front of her, and with the back of his hand gently brushed the tear from her cheek.

"Once, when I was a young naval officer, I met a little girl in a lighthouse who stole my heart."

Katie closed her eyes as another tear escaped, then opened them as Max gently cupped her face in his hands.

"She was my *keeper girl* until her wicked aunt tried to

keep us apart. So I did the only thing a reputable developer could do under the circumstances, I bought her a light station."

Tears streamed down Katie's face.

"If you only knew," he said as he lowered his hands to her shoulders, "what lengths I've gone through to get your attention." He slanted her an ironic glance. "Do you have any idea how much money I had to donate to the Sheriff's Ball to get him to go along with that community service thing?"

Katie began to cry in earnest and that was all the excuse Max needed as he folded her in his arms.

"Oh, Katie, please don't cry. You're breaking my heart."

"You mean to tell me that you loved me all this time and that the station is mine." She bubbled up with laughter. Max scooped her up and carried her to the chair, tucking her comfortably in his lap. He reached into his pocket and pulled out an envelope she immediately recognized. The look he gave Katie threatened to melt her bones. In sheer joy, she threw her arms around him.

"I never dreamed you'd actually get it," she said in muffled tones against his sweater.

Max looked down at her, his smile wreaking havoc with her quivering nerves and her racing pulse. A tender hand lifted her face from his chest. "I almost didn't. I had just about quit checking that old post office box of mine. And you were right, by the way. I did come to see you. You were also right about your aunt's response to my visit. But Katie, there's something I have to tell you right here and now."

"I never blamed you for that accident," she said, halting him in his tracks. "I know you were the one with Davy. It's all there in my letters to you. Of course, at the time I wrote them, I had no idea you and Davy's Annapolis friend were the same person. Your actions saved a boy's life that day. And Davy wouldn't have had it any other way." Katie lowered his head to hers, giving him her sweetest kiss.

"Oh, Katie. Thank you for that," he said, his voice clogged with emotion as he hugged her close. "I thought Margaret might act differently toward me since it had been years since Davy's accident, but she still blamed me as before and assured me you felt the same. I was worried she was right because your letters had stopped coming. But when I saw your reaction to finding them, I knew differently."

"How long have you known, Max? And what do you mean you bought the light station for me? Tell me everything." The words tumbled out with babbling delight.

"I've known ever since we introduced ourselves that first night in the cottage. Then I recognized the picture of you and Davy and that pretty much sealed it."

"You've known since then?"

He nodded.

"So you knew who I was that day in the tower?"

He nodded again.

"No wonder you were so sure of yourself."

"Well, you did ask me to kiss you," he said as he patted her letter, now tucked back in his breast pocket. "And I have to say I did my *very* best not to disappoint you," he added with a grin. "And from then on, I tried every tactical maneuver I could think of to get your attention, some of them quite costly."

"Oh, Max, why didn't you just tell me who you were?" Katie asked, lifting appealing eyes up at him. "I feel like we've wasted so much time."

"Angel, no time spent with you has ever been wasted." He planted a firm, possessive kiss on her mouth. "Besides, your reception of me wasn't the most encouraging, although I can't blame you, considering the circumstances. Plus you and I both had preconceived notions about each other. I knew I wasn't the same person you met in the tower all those years ago, and as for you ..." He rolled his eyes heavenward. "Here I thought I was returning to my sweet tower girl, only to be met with a maddening, but very beautiful creature whose wayward tendencies, I might add, had me alarmed on more than one occasion. So, as any commanding officer worth his salt would do, I retreated to reassess the situation."

"You could have at least given me a hint." She grabbed the front of his jacket, giving him a good shake.

"Oh, I gave you plenty, angel. You were just too busy arguing." He smiled indulgently at her.

"It's not fair. All this time you knew I was me, but I didn't know you were you."

Max threw back his head and laughed. "Who says the game of love has to be fair?" He cocked a wicked grin at her. "I had the advantage, and that's all I cared about."

"How did you find out that I was the other bidder?"

"You don't really think I could live in a town the size of Paige Point and not find out all about you. Remember when I told you that you were everyone's darling? You are, you know."

"Just as long as I'm yours," she said.

Max lowered his lips to hers, the passion and strength of him crushing in its intensity, giving her all the answer she needed.

Some time later, Max raised his head and entwined his fingers in her silky hair.

"Katie, that day I picked up the plungers, I ran into Tom at Paul's Deli. Since I had just had a rather informative talk with Lily, I thought I'd pump Tom for some more answers. And boy did I get plenty. Talk about feeling like an interloper. I was completely floored, and here I was reupholstering your parents' furniture. But it was the night of our party when Tom told me you were the other bidder. God, when I learned of the sacrifices you made. Do you realize how remarkable you are?" He cupped her face with his hands. "I can only imagine how much I hurt you. When I think of how Henry Davis and the rest of that blasted council took advantage of you. Believe me, I wanted to hang every one of them from the yardarm."

Katie drew his face down to hers and placed her lips tenderly against his frowning ones, moving over them in tantalizing sweetness until his frown disappeared and his lips formed a roguish grin.

"And when I think how angry you were with me at times," she said. "I guess I should be thankful it was only *threats and custody* for me," she teased against his lips.

"I can see you never looked up the word," he admonished with a definite teasing light in his eye.

Katie cocked her head to one side. "Oh, I looked it up all right, then slammed the dictionary shut, if you must know."

"Ah, then you must not have read far enough." He began covering her face with feather-light kisses. "Or you would have come to words like care, safekeeping, and protection. So, were you really going to walk out and leave all of your worldly goods at the station?" he asked, his mouth warm against her lips.

"You already had my heart, so what were a few odds and ends like the family silver?" Katie pulled away and slid her hands down to his chest. "Besides," she said, now fingering a button on his sweater. "I figured you and Miss Batson could have them as a wedding present."

"What is this fetish you have with Sal?"

"I thought you were engaged to her."

"You must indeed think I'm a dark horse if you think I could kiss you while engaged to another. But I can see I'll have to convince you otherwise." He pulled her firmly against his chest.

"Max." It took all of Katie's resolve to push him away

before giving him one of her quelling looks. "I saw her kiss you."

Max looked a bit confused.

"You were with Nate and some older man at the Inn. I—I watched you through a window."

"You were there? Good heavens, no wonder you were confused. That little celebration you witnessed was in honor of Nate and Sal's engagement. And as I recall, Sal did indeed kiss me, but as her future brother-in-law." Max paused, waiting for his words to sink in.

"She's marrying Nate?"

"Uh huh. But we also raised a toast to *finally* finding ... Katherine Clare," he said, looking at her with a gleam of anticipation in his eye.

"Katherine Clare?"

"Sal recognized the drawing you gave me for Christmas."

"How could she recognize it? You mean? Wait a minute." She shot to her feet. "You're Falcon Designs?"

"Guilty as charged. Falcon is, after all, my middle name."

"You're her boss."

"Guilty again."

"And just why did you back out on the deal for my paintings? Sally loved them, so it must have been you." She felt moisture prickle the edges of her eyes, but she refused to let him see how much he'd hurt her by rejecting her artwork.

Max stood. "Katie, it's not what you think."

"Have you any idea what I went through to get those paintings finished on time?" Aggravation soaked her voice as she stopped her pacing to throw up her arms in the air. "Oh, when I think of the nights I had to sneak out after everyone was asleep! Oh no, I couldn't paint them under normal circumstances." Her voice rose on a shrill note. "Heaven forbid I should leave the painters and the plumbers."

As Katie continued to rant, Max flicked back the cuff on his sweater and glanced at his watch. When he'd had enough, he stepped toward her and clamped his fingers over her lips, shutting her up.

"Months? You want to hear about months? I spent that and then some looking for Katherine Clare just to find out she was none other than this annoying little termagant that I was madly in love with. Also, if you think I'm going to have my future wife's artwork hanging in any of Peter Markesan's hotels, when they can be hanging in ours, you can think again."

Max gave her a look that dared her to speak. "Come here," he said drawing her none too gently into his arms. "How you can be snuggly one second then ranting the next is beyond me!"

"F—future wife?"

Her eyes glistened as she gazed up at his face, but just as suddenly, her forehead creased.

"That's not a very romantic proposal."

He gave her a wry smile. "I was planning to propose to you last night."

"Oh."

Max hugged her to him, dispelling any and all disappointment, then led her over to stand before the fire.

"Marry me, Katie." It was not a question.

"Yes, oh yes." She flung her arms around his neck and clung to him.

Max laughed and wrapped his arms around her. His breath was warm against her hair. "Obedience at last."

"Don't let it go to your head, mister."

"You mean master," Max said as his lips claimed hers in possessive hunger.

The low clouds caught and held the deep orangey-red hues that pulled like taffy along the horizon.

"You're gonna' miss it." Katie leaned forward over the rail and yelled down at Max as he made his way across the winter lawn to the lighthouse door. Even from this distance, she took note of his broad shoulders that filled out his thick wool fisherman's sweater to perfection. Katie glanced down at the heart-shaped engagement ring that sparkled up from her hand. She smiled as she recalled what he'd said as he slipped it on her finger ... *since you have a fondness for hearts.*

She heard the door open behind her and felt a pair of strong arms wrap around her waist. In sheer happiness, Katie leaned back comfortably and securely against his powerful frame, then tilted her head upward to receive his kiss.

"You almost missed it."

"I've seen sunsets before," he said with a contented sigh as he hugged her close.

"Not with me in your arms, you haven't. And if you keep looking at me, sir, you will miss it."

"I prefer watching how the sun dances off your beautiful face," he said, his voice husky. He placed a kiss on the nape of her neck.

Katie turned slightly in his arms in order to look up at him. "I love you, Max."

"I love you more. Now kiss me," he demanded as he lowered his head to hers, laying claim to her lips in a kiss that promised years of sunsets together.

CPSIA information can be obtained at www.ICGtesting.com
Printed in the USA
LVOW071139101212

310853LV00001B/1/P